Point of No Return

Point of No Return

Paul McCusker

PUBLISHING
Colorado Springs, Colorado

POINT OF NO RETURN
Copyright © 1995 by Focus on the Family. All rights reserved. International copyright
secured.

Library of Congress Cataloging-in-Publication Data

McCusker, Paul, 1958–
    Point of no return/Paul McCusker.
       p. cm. — (Adventures in Odyssey; 8)
    Summary: Ten-year-old Jimmy Barclay thinks his life will be much better after he
says yes to Jesus, so when he loses his best friend and his grandmother dies, Jimmy
wonders if becoming a Christian was the right thing to do.
    ISBN 1-56179-401-5
    [1. Christian life—Fiction. 2. Behavior—Fiction. 3. Family life—Fiction.
4. Friendship—Fiction.] I. Title. II. Series: McCusker, Paul, 1958- Adventures in
Odyssey; 8.
PZ7.M47841635Po 1995
[Fic]—dc20   95-19068
                                                 CIP
                                               AC

Published by Focus on the Family Publishing, Colorado Springs, CO 80995.
Distributed in the U.S.A. and Canada by Word Books, Dallas, Texas.

Front cover illustration: Jeff Haynie

Printed in the United States of America
96 97 98 99/10 9 8 7 6 5 4 3

to
Matt and Sam Butcher

*Fans of the audio and video series
of **Adventures in Odyssey** may wonder why some
of their favorite characters aren't found in these
novels. The answer is simple: the novels take
place in a period of time prior
to the audio or video series.*

CHAPTER ONE

Friday Night

J immy Barclay looked into the deep blue water. It was still. Faintly, he could see his reflection looking back. It didn't look much like him, though. In fact, it could have been a complete stranger . . . but it wasn't. That had to be his young face looking up out of the water. The blue, still water.

There was also the scent of pine.

He got on his knees and looked closer at the deep blue water—pondering it. He waited.

This was really stupid, he knew. At his age—a mature and wise 10 years old—he shouldn't be in this situation. He never should've let Tony talk him into it. How many kids of 10 try to smoke their best friend's father's cigar? What made it worse was that Jimmy thought people who smoked cigarettes were Neanderthals. So why did he try the cigar?

He rested his head against the porcelain, sending a tiny shiver through the toilet bowl. The deep blue water rippled. The scent of pine was overpowering. *Mom must have cleaned in here today*, he thought. He couldn't imagine when, though. His mother worked part-time as a dental receptionist and was on every committee the church could think up.

A new wave of nausea worked its way through Jimmy's stomach, and he prepared himself for it. Again, he stared into the deep blue water. Again, it was so still.

At that moment, he tried to remember how many puffs he had taken on the cigar before Tony said he was turning green. He couldn't remember. Too many. Way too many.

The wave subsided, and he sat down. He rested his head against the cabinet that housed the sink and prayed for deliverance. He begged his stomach to make up its mind: *Either do it or don't do it. Let's stop playing around.*

Of course, I wish you wouldn't *do it*, Jimmy told his stomach.

From his room down the hall, he could hear music. Tony, his best friend, was listening to—singing along with—some rock album he had brought over. Jimmy winced. It sounded as if Tony had the stereo turned up full blast.

Jimmy wondered how long it would be before Donna, his older sister, would hang up the phone downstairs and yell at him to turn off the stereo. He thought about hollering for Tony to turn it down but was afraid to. He didn't know what it would do to his stomach or his mother's freshly cleaned bathroom.

He leaned over the deep blue water again just in case.

Tony screamed along with a song.

How could he be so energetic when Jimmy was sitting on the bathroom floor ready to die? Easy. Tony was good at talking Jimmy into doing stupid things and never doing them himself.

Jimmy grabbed the sides of the bowl, sure that something was about to happen. He held on and waited.

This is so very very very dumb. When will you learn? When will you stop acting like such an idiot? You're a jerk, Jimmy Barclay, and you'd better never let this happen again.

As if to say it agreed, his stomach settled down. It seemed suddenly at peace.

After a moment, Jimmy stood up slowly. His head swayed a little. He dropped the cover over the deep blue water and turned to the door. Everything would be just fine.

He paused at the mirror and looked hard at himself. *A little green around the gills maybe—but nothing too terrible. Just Jimmy Barclay looking a little sick. Boy, it's a good thing Mom and Dad are out.*

He opened the door, turned out the light, and headed for his room. He didn't notice that the music had stopped. It didn't click in his mind that all was deathly silent. When he entered his room to find Tony sitting quietly on the edge of his bed, he still didn't think much of it . . .

Until he saw his mom at his stereo and his dad looking over the remains of the cigar.

There are no words to describe the look on their faces—but

most children know it when they see it. Jimmy knew it well. His stomach turned upside down, and he considered running back to the bathroom.

"Get ready for bed, Jimmy," his dad said as he walked out of the room with the cigar. His mom looked at him with an expression of complete disappointment and followed.

And that was it.

Jimmy looked at Tony.

Tony shrugged and said, "I didn't hear them coming. I would have done something if I knew they were coming."

"How could you hear them with the tape going full blast?" Jimmy asked. "They probably heard it at the restaurant and came home to investigate."

His dad yelled from the kitchen, "Do you need a lift home, Tony?"

Tony looked at Jimmy. Jimmy shrugged.

Tony shouted back, "Oh, no thanks. I'd better walk."

"Good night, then," Mrs. Barclay called out.

"I guess that means I'm leaving now," Tony said to Jimmy, grabbing his jacket from the foot of the bed.

"I guess so."

"See ya," Tony said as he drifted out of the room. "Call me when you get paroled."

"Thanks, *pal*."

Tony opened the front door and called out a final farewell to Mr. and Mrs. Barclay before retreating into the crisp Friday night.

Jimmy sighed.

From somewhere on the front lawn, Jimmy could hear an outburst of Tony's laughter.

*****

George Barclay, Jimmy's dad, was sitting at the kitchen table drinking coffee. Mary, Jimmy's mom, was at the counter pouring herself a cup. Donna also sat at the table with a stricken look on her face. Obviously, his mom and dad had already read her the riot act. Jimmy guessed that they held her partly to blame for what had happened. She had been on the phone when she should have been keeping a closer eye on him.

"You're home early," Jimmy said brightly.

After a moment of silence, his dad spoke. "We're home early because I decided to go see your grandmother tomorrow. I may leave first thing in the morning."

Grandma Barclay was Jimmy's dad's mom. She had been sick over the past couple of weeks, and they were worried it might be a relapse of her cancer. She lived a couple of hundred miles away.

"Oh—you're going by yourself?"

His dad looked darkly at him and said, "Your mother was going to come with me, but it's clear that we can't leave the two of you alone."

Guilt poked at Jimmy's stomach. "I can go with you," he offered.

"No, you can't." His dad looked Jimmy full in the face

now. *That* look was still there. "You're on restriction. For the rest of your life. Maybe longer. And when we get a minute, your mother and I are going to talk about what to do with you. I can't figure which is worse: the fact that you lit matches in your room or the fact that you tried smoking a *cigar*. Maybe they're equal. And there's Tony coming tonight when we told you before we left that you weren't to have friends in. And that music you were playing at a speaker-blowing volume. Not forgetting to mention the water balloon battle you had in my study *last* weekend, the fire you started in the garage with the blowtorch the week before, the call we got from the librarian about you and Tony knocking books off the shelves, the fight you had with Kelly next door over that bike, and, and . . . Jimmy—"

He stopped as if his anger had tied up his tongue. "Just go to bed," he finally said.

*****

In his room, Jimmy began unloading his pants pockets. It was something he always did before undressing and going to bed because, if he didn't, his mom might accidentally wash something important like coins, a crumpled dollar, some gum he had bought at Town Center Drugs, lint . . .

So much for the left pocket. He emptied the right. More lint.

He tossed everything onto his dresser, where his eye caught the framed photo of Grandma Barclay. She'd lost a lot of weight since that picture was taken. The cancer did it. It had been eating her alive a few years ago, but everyone prayed for her, and it went into remission. Jimmy wasn't so sure prayer had made her better, but he didn't dare say so out loud.

You wouldn't know how ill Grandma was if you saw only the picture with its soft-focus close-up that made her wrinkles less noticeable, gave a nice shine to her white hair, and accented her bright blue eyes. They were stunning eyes, the kind that made Jimmy feel funny because he suspected they could somehow see much deeper than eyes should be allowed to see.

Grandma Barclay was a very devout woman. As far as anyone knew, she had never missed a day of church in her life. Hers was a deep-rooted, practical faith. It was as real and natural to her as breathing. Jimmy's father felt the influence of that faith and tried to instill it in both Jimmy and Donna. Donna liked church. Jimmy thought it was boring. He would've stopped going if his parents didn't make him attend. He once talked to them about letting him stay home, but they wouldn't hear of it. He had to go, and that was that.

Jimmy's parents fussed with him for a while about his lack of faith. They did everything they could to get him interested. But lately it was as if they had given up on him. His mom said that they had decided to stop worrying and let God do the rest.

That was fine with Jimmy, because God seemed to want to leave him alone, too.

Grandma didn't fuss about it at all. When she found out Jimmy didn't like church, she just smiled and said he would enjoy it eventually. *He would have to. The call in his life was too strong.*

Jimmy didn't know what she meant by that. He wondered but didn't want to risk a lecture by asking. He got off easy, and that's all that mattered.

But sometimes he thought about *the call* and tried to figure out what a call would sound like. Not that it would make any difference. When Jimmy grew up, he wanted to be a singer in a rock-and-roll band.

All these thoughts swirled around in his churning mind as he fell asleep. The last thing he would remember was the sound of thousands of fans cheering him as he performed in a huge auditorium.

CHAPTER TWO

Saturday Morning

The October sun played peekaboo with Jimmy's left eyelid through the crack between the half-drawn curtains on his bedroom window. Swimming to the surface of wakefulness, he was aware of the irritation the sunlight caused him. He moved his head. The sunlight hit his right eyelid. He moved his head again. Relief.

But not for long.

Right on cue, his head throbbed. He rolled over with a groan and tried to open his mouth to lick the cobwebs off his lips. His tongue felt like a fuzzball. His eyes twitched but wouldn't open. He was numb all over.

He rolled over onto his back again and rubbed at his eyes until they could open.

His room looked as if someone had hung a giant piece of

gauze over it. He blinked. The gauze separated like a curtain, and he made out the specifics—so familiar and so cluttered. Posters covered almost every inch of wall space. The small desk was piled high with magazines, school papers, comic books, and only heaven knew what else. The closet was an outpouring of clean and dirty clothes, games, games, and more games. A chair was covered with more clothes. A small table held his stereo and surrounding stacks of cassette tapes. And there was the ancient oak dresser with the Old West wagon train lamp and 96-ounce beer mug half filled with pennies. Also on top, as a testimony to the night before, was the junk he had taken out of his pockets last night.

He moaned as he remembered what had happened.

He remembered Tony, the cigar, deep blue water, and ... his parents coming home.

He scanned the room, trying to remember where he threw his alarm clock. He had no idea what time it might be. He sat up, and his head protested.

As he struggled to get out of bed, the door slowly opened, and Donna peeked in. She looked annoyed until she saw Jimmy swing his legs off the side of the bed.

"Mom wants to know if you want some breakfast," she asked.

He shook his head. "Maybe later" was all he could manage. His tongue wouldn't let go of the roof of his mouth. After a moment he asked, "What time is it?"

"Almost lunchtime." She retreated.

"Donna?"

She returned and said, "What?"

He hesitated, then: "Are Mom and Dad . . . still mad?"

"What do you think?" she asked and left again.

He gingerly stepped out of bed and grabbed at the nearest stack of clothes.

*****

In the bathroom, Jimmy tried to use water to flatten some of his hair. It stuck out in 12 directions. He looked at his face. His eyes looked tiny. He leaned closer to the mirror and checked his chin and top lip for anything that might look like a beard. He couldn't wait until he was old enough to shave.

Grabbing the skeletal remains of a bar of soap, he scrubbed his hands. And he began to think—not the way the world's great thinkers do, but with all the concentration he could manage. He replayed the night before in his mind and wondered what made him act the way he did.

He searched his mind for something or someone to blame. Blank.

Nothing.

He did what he did because it was what he *wanted* to do. That was all. There really wasn't any other reason, was there?

Something was just out of reach in his mind. A thought, a feeling . . . he wasn't sure. But it made him feel that something was wrong. Maybe something was wrong with *him*. Maybe he should try harder to behave himself. Maybe he should change somehow.

But he was only 10 years old. What could be wrong with him at the age of 10? How much can a 10-year-old be expected to change? He shrugged and walked out of the bathroom.

*****

Mary Barclay sat silently at the table drinking a cup of tea. Jimmy halfheartedly ate some sugar-coated cereal that promised to be part of a nutritious breakfast. His head still sent dull thuds to his eyes. Did cigars make everybody feel so bad?

His dad had gone to Jimmy's grandma's house. It didn't really sink into Jimmy's mind what was happening, but someone called that morning to say his grandmother was in great pain and had to be put back in the hospital, and the doctors were playing guessing games about radiation and maybe chemo, but there were no promises, no guarantees, because she was almost 80 years old and not as strong as she used to be.

His mother looked Jimmy directly in the eyes and asked, "Why, Jimmy? Why do you get into so much trouble? The past few months have been one incident after another. Last night was the last straw. Why do you do it?"

His mouth was full of sugar-coated cereal, so he couldn't answer her.

"I wanted to see your grandma, too, but . . ." She looked down at her cup of tea. "I can't trust you anymore."

Jimmy swallowed hard. He could tell by her tone that she wasn't just trying to make him feel guilty. She wasn't even trying to make him feel bad. She was speaking in a neutral voice as if she were telling him about the weather. That made it even worse. Jimmy searched frantically for the right words to say—something to convince her he could be trustworthy.

He couldn't think of anything. So finally he offered, "I'm sorry, Mom. I just got carried away. It won't happen again."

The words sounded hollow even as he said them.

"That's what you keep saying over and over."

"This time I mean it," he said, on the edge of pleading. All his life there had been a bond of trust between him and his parents. Even when he misbehaved, the bond somehow stood firm. To lose it, to feel he had truly failed them, was more than he could handle. "I'll behave."

"Don't tell me you'll behave. I know better. You feel bad this morning, but that won't last. You'll get with Tony and forget."

He stood up to take his dishes to the sink. "It's not Tony's fault," he said. He stood there, looking out the window into the backyard. The swings on the swing set moved gently in a breeze.

"I'm not blaming Tony. He's been like another son in this family. But he *does* influence you. You can't deny that."

He turned back to face her and said, "Maybe I'm influencing *him*."

She took a drink of her tea. "I hope not," she replied. "I hope I raised you better than that. But since you got bored with church . . ." Her voice faded, the sentence left unfinished.

Jimmy knew where the conversation was going. He closed

his eyes. He didn't want to talk about that. He wanted to go out.

"You say you'll behave, and then you don't. I don't think you *can* behave by yourself. I think you need help." She watched him as she spoke. "So, until further notice, Tony can't come over, and you can't sleep over at his house. You're on restriction. And that means you have to come straight home from school—no Tony, no Whit's End, nothing."

Jimmy's jaw tightened, and he looked away. He hadn't expected his punishment to be *that* bad.

Just then, somebody knocked at the front door.

Mary stood up, saying as she walked out of the kitchen, "I want you to think about how you behave and what it does to us . . . *all* of us. Another night like last night and I . . . I don't know what we'll do."

Jimmy brooded as he listened to his mom walk to the front door and open it. Probably the mailman with a personal delivery, he figured.

"Ever since you got bored with church . . ." she had said to him. *Church, church, church*, he moaned inwardly. Church was the last thing he needed. He knew plenty of people who went to church, and they weren't any better than him. In fact, he could think of a whole list of people who seemed worse off because of church.

"Jimmy," his mom called from the living room, "there's someone here to see you."

Huh? he thought. *Who in the world would come to see me in the middle of a Saturday except Tony?* He pushed off from the sink and rounded the corner into the living room. It might have been his imagination, but he thought he could still smell the cigar somewhere.

That's when Dave Wright and his son, Jacob, entered Jimmy's life.

Dave was the ever-smiling, ever-friendly kids' pastor from Calvary Church—his family's church. Jimmy had heard of him and seen him in the pulpit to make announcements, but he stayed clear of him whenever he could. But there he stood, right in Jimmy's own living room, grinning from ear to ear. His 10-year-old son, Jacob, stood next to him with the same smile. Jimmy's mom stood next to them both.

It was a setup. A trap.

"I'll go to the kitchen to make some tea," she said and quickly departed.

Dave stepped forward, hand outstretched. "I'm Dave Wright from Calvary."

Jimmy hesitated and then shook his hand. His grip was firm. *Obviously a barbell boy*, Jimmy thought. *That's a surprise. Most of the church leaders I've ever met turned out to be meek, mousy, turn-the-other-cheek types.* "Hi," Jimmy said.

"This is my son, Jacob," Dave said.

Jimmy nodded to Jacob. Kids their age didn't shake hands unless they were making a deal.

"I've heard a lot about you, Jimmy," Dave said. He moved to the couch to sit down.

"Oh," Jimmy said, bugged that Dave sat down. That meant

he planned to stay for a little while. Jacob leaned against the side of the couch.

"You're wondering why we're here, right?" Dave asked, then gestured to the end table. "I had to drop off some Sunday school material for your mom."

Jimmy glanced down skeptically at a couple of Sunday school books sitting there.

Dave chuckled and said, "Actually, that's a lie. I really came by to talk to you."

"Isn't it a sin to lie?" Jimmy asked.

"Yeah, it is," Dave said with mock shame. "I guess that's why I'm still just a kids' pastor. I'll graduate to pastor when I can stop sinning."

Jimmy looked at him blankly.

Dave's smile faded. "I'm kidding," he explained.

This guy is really weird, Jimmy thought. He was wearing a normal-looking sportcoat and tie and had longish brown hair, a plain face, and an athlete's build. He wasn't at all what Jimmy thought a kids' pastor should be. Kids' pastors were supposed to be wimps. Even Jacob looked like his father, except he was too young to lift weights.

"I have to go now, okay?" Jimmy said as he moved toward the stairs. "My mom's in the kitchen if you want to talk to her some more."

"Wait a sec," Dave said, waving him back. "What's the problem? We're here to talk to you."

Jimmy stopped. "Yeah, and I know what you wanna talk

about, and I don't wanna talk about it, okay? I don't like church."

Dave laughed. "I know," he said. "Sometimes I don't like it either."

"I guess that makes us even." Jimmy faked a smile and turned away to head for his room.

"How does that make us even? I still want to talk to you." Dave stood up and followed Jimmy. He obviously wasn't going to let Jimmy go without a fight.

"About what?" Jimmy asked.

"I want to know why you don't like church."

"I don't know. It's boring, that's all. No offense."

"No offense? Are you kidding? What have I said, what have I done?" Dave pretended he was hurt. "It's my breath, isn't it? Go on. You can be straight with me."

At the top of the stairs, Jimmy stopped. "It doesn't have anything to do with you." This guy really was a wacko.

"Then you have something against the church?"

"I just don't care, okay?" He went into his room, hoping Dave and Jacob would go away.

But they didn't. Dave and Jacob stepped into the room. Jimmy felt invaded—it was *his* room, for crying out loud. Why wouldn't these guys go away? Jimmy looked for something he could busy himself with.

Dave smiled and continued, "You're evading the question, Jimmy. I want to know what *your problem is*."

"I don't know!" Jimmy said.

"Not an acceptable answer. Try again."

Jimmy felt uneasy. "What is this—a quiz?"

Dave smiled. "Sort of," he said. "Why don't you come to the church youth club?"

"'Cause I don't feel like it." It was all he could think of.

"Not acceptable. You're oh for two." Dave frowned and shook a finger at him. "You're flunking, Jimmy."

Jimmy was tongue-tied. He didn't know how to get out of this. But he had to say *something* . . . so, he grunted.

"I'm sorry," Dave said, "was that a grunt?"

"Yes, it was. Do you want me to do it again?" And he did.

Dave laughed. "That's the most intelligent thing you've said so far."

Jimmy sighed and said, "What do you want from me? What's it gonna take? Do you wanna hear my life story? I could tell you a lot. I could make up even more."

"I'll bet you could."

"What do you want to know? Just ask."

"I did, and you grunted. I'm afraid of what you might do if I ask anything harder." Dave sat down on Jimmy's unmade bed and leaned forward, his elbows on his knees. "I want you to come to one of our club meetings. Just one." His voice was low and very serious.

Jimmy grimaced. "And do what? Drink punch? Sing some boring folk songs? Pray?"

"Maybe."

"Forget it," Jimmy said firmly and glanced at Jacob, who seemed to be admiring some of his posters. It bothered Jimmy that Jacob didn't speak.

For a second, Dave seemed at a loss for words. But only a second. "That's it? There's nothing I can do to get you to come?"

"You can tie me up and drag me, I guess," Jimmy said.

Jimmy knew right away that it was the wrong thing to suggest. Dave looked as if he might consider the idea. Instead, however, he stood up and offered, "How about a deal?"

Jimmy cocked an eyebrow. "What kind of deal?"

"What sports do you play?"

"I don't know. Most of them." Jimmy looked at him suspiciously. "What kind of deal?"

"Pick a sport."

Jimmy eyed him, trying to figure out what he was up to. "A sport?"

"I saw a basketball hoop over the garage. You use it?" Even as Dave asked, he began taking off his sportcoat.

"Me and my dad play sometimes. Why? What are you going to do?"

Dave knelt down and tightened his shoelaces. "We'll play one on one. First to reach 10 wins." He untied his tie and pulled it off. "You lose and you'll have to come to the club meeting."

"Play *you?*" Jimmy laughed. "No way."

"Don't be silly," Dave said. "I'll just referee. You'll play against Jacob."

Jacob looked at Jimmy without smiling. Jimmy realized Jacob stood about an inch shorter than himself. "And if I win?"

"We won't nag you ever again," Dave said with a smile.

"That doesn't sound like much of a deal."

Dave laughed and said, "You've never seen us really nag."

Jimmy sized up Jacob and thought about his chances of winning.

"Well?" Dave asked.

"I don't know . . ." Jimmy ran his fingers through his short, curly hair, his habit when thinking hard.

"They call me the Hound of Heaven," Dave said. "I'll stay on your tracks for the rest of your life. For eternity."

Jimmy looked at him closely. This situation had all the elements of a "Twilight Zone" episode. But this was a dare, a challenge. It intrigued him too much not to see it through to the end. "I'm gonna regret this," Jimmy finally said. "Deal."

Jacob and Jimmy silently shook hands.

Dave smiled again and moved to the door. "I have a ball in the car," he said. "Let's go."

Jimmy dug under his bed to get his basketball shoes. He tried to figure his chances of winning. Jacob was shorter and looked a little wimpy. Jimmy, on the other hand, considered himself a pretty good basketball player—not because he loved the game, but because he played against his dad. It would be a good match. And as Jimmy put on his shoes, he psyched himself up. He told himself all the reasons why he would win. Why he *had to* win.

Jimmy's mom caught him at the bottom of the stairs. She asked what was going on. Outside, Jimmy heard Jacob dribbling the basketball on the driveway. "I just moved the car so you could play . . . basketball?"

Jimmy explained the deal.

She shook her head. "I don't like it," she said. "I don't like it at all."

"You're right," Jimmy agreed, "it's risky. Jacob could win."

"That's not what I'm afraid of." She turned and walked away.

Thanks, Mom, he thought. *Glad to have you in the cheering section.*

CHAPTER THREE

Early Saturday Afternoon

Before long, Jimmy was leading off with three baskets. Then he made four and five before Jacob got his first. *Piece a cake*, Jimmy thought even as the midday sun bore down and his pace slackened. His lead slackened, too. Jacob got two more baskets. Then—after a long stretch where neither scored—Jacob got another one.

"Jimmy: five; Jacob: four!" Dave announced from the side.

What bugged Jimmy the most was Jacob's silence. He never said a word: no jokes, commentary, or exclamations that were usually part of the game. It was killing Jimmy's concentration.

Donna stood off to the side, watching with delight. She screamed and cheered . . . for Jacob.

"Get lost, Donna!" Jimmy shouted at her.

Then it was Jimmy: five; Jacob: five.

Good going, Jimmy, he thought. *Give the poor kid a false sense of security.*

Jimmy pushed his inner power button and got two more baskets in rapid-fire succession.

"Whoa," Dave cried out, "maybe we should've challenged you to darts."

Mrs. Barclay brought a round of drinks, giving both Dave and Jimmy a disapproving glance as she served them. She didn't like this one bit. She said so again.

Back to the game.

Jimmy stole the ball from Jacob and shot from halfway down the driveway. Jimmy: eight; Jacob: five.

They traded baskets after they both alternately knocked the ball out of bounds. Then it was Jimmy: nine; Jacob: six.

One more basket and it would be all over. Jacob, still silent, breathed hard and looked tired. Jimmy figured he couldn't lose. The thought gave him a shot of adrenaline, and he plowed through for an almost-perfect layup. *Almost* perfect. He missed.

Jacob rebounded, recovered, and scored. To Jimmy's irritation, he then snatched the ball from Jimmy and scored again.

Jimmy: nine; Jacob: eight.

Jimmy went up again, with style and grace, and fired a shot. It hit the basket and rolled around and around. And around. And out.

"I've been robbed!" Jimmy cried.

Jacob got a swisher to tie things up.

The excitement and tension were at their peak. Donna could barely contain herself.

"Why don't you go find a friend or something?" Jimmy growled at her. This wasn't right. It wasn't fair. He'd had the lead most of the game, and he should have made those last two baskets with no problem. He looked at Jacob and said, "No fair if you're praying."

For the first time, Jacob made a sound. He laughed. Dave laughed with him. And while they laughed, Jimmy realized he liked them both.

That was a good thing, because Jimmy went up for another shot knowing full well that this time it would be perfect, and he would get the basket and win and not be at the mercy of this lunatic father-and-son team that he liked in spite of his better senses. And there it was—the ball at the very tips of his fingers, reaching up and up and up toward the basket, and all he had to do was let go and it would be in, and . . .

Then Jacob was up with him, jumping higher than Jimmy would have ever imagined someone of his size jumping. In that instant, Jimmy remembered reading about a guy from a nearby college who was known as the "Thieving Kangaroo" because he could jump high and steal the ball from anybody, and his name was Dave Wright, and he had given up his future in basketball to go into the ministry.

That's when Jimmy lost—no, he *quit*—because he realized he'd never had a chance to begin with and that Jacob had inherited his dad's jumping ability and natural talent and probably could have slaughtered him at any time.

Sure enough, Jacob knocked the ball away and, in less than a minute, scored and won.

"You didn't tell me who you were," Jimmy panted as they all walked back into the house.

"You didn't ask," was Dave's reply.

CHAPTER FOUR

Late Saturday Afternoon

Jimmy sat on the edge of his bed and fingered the small booklet Dave and Jacob had left with him. He didn't read it. He simply turned it over and over absentmindedly while he tried to come up with a good excuse to go back on his word and skip the youth club meeting that night. At the moment, his only ploy was that it was unfair for Dave and Jacob to lure him into a basketball game when Jacob was the son of a great player. *No, that won't work*, he decided.

Maybe he could come down with something contagious.

Jimmy's plotting was interrupted by a tap at his window. Tony sat on a tree branch outside looking like the serpent in the Garden of Eden. Jimmy opened his window.

"Hey, Jimmy," Tony said as casually as if he were sitting on the living room sofa instead of an unsteady branch.

"Get out of here or I'll get in worse trouble than I already am," Jimmy said.

Tony smiled as he asked, "Did your mom and dad give it to you good?"

"You know they did," Jimmy said. "They were really ticked off, and you're not supposed to be here."

"That's too bad. You're gonna miss a great time tonight."

Jimmy frowned. "Tonight? What's going on tonight?"

"A couple of us are going out to Allen's Pond. I heard that a bunch of Nathan's friends are gonna get drunk and stuff." Nathan was Tony's older brother and did things like sneak out and get drunk. He hated Tony and Jimmy for hanging around, but they did it anyway.

Jimmy thought of how fun it'd be to follow Nathan and his pals like a couple of secret agents on a mission. But he knew he couldn't—not tonight of all nights. "I can't anyway," he said. "I have to go to church."

"Church!" Tony nearly fell out of the tree.

"Yeah. I got tricked into going."

"But it's not Sunday! Why're you going to church on a Saturday night?"

Jimmy toyed with the booklet he still held in his hand. "Because that's when the kids get together. I guess it's kinda like a Saturday night Sunday school."

"Oh boy! I wish I could go with you!" Tony said in the singsong voice he used to tease Jimmy.

"Why don't you?" Jimmy asked seriously. "Then maybe

I won't get so bored."

Tony scowled at Jimmy. "You're kidding."

"No."

"Forget it," Tony said.

"Thanks, *friend*," Jimmy said and closed the window.

Tony laughed as he slithered down the tree branch and out of Jimmy's sight.

Jimmy sat down on his bed again and looked at the booklet. "If you were to die tonight . . ." the black letters on the front said. Jimmy had seen the booklet before in a rack in the lobby of his church. He had never paid attention to it. Why should he? At his age, why would he think about death? Kids his age didn't die unless they were in car accidents or got some kind of weird disease. And Jimmy didn't plan on getting in any car accidents or coming down with a weird disease— unless it would get him out of going to that meeting at church. What did death have to do with him? Death happened to other people that Jimmy didn't know. Death happened in the make-believe world of movies. Death happened to old people.

That last thought gave him an uneasy feeling as his grandmother came to mind. She was old and sick. She might even die. What would happen to her after that? She always told Jimmy she wasn't afraid of death. Because of Jesus, she knew she would go to heaven. Jimmy believed her. She *would* go to heaven because she was the best grandmother anybody could ever have.

"If you were to die tonight . . ." the booklet said.

It wasn't talking about Jimmy's grandmother. It was talking to Jimmy.

He threw the booklet onto his nightstand. *What a stupid idea*, he thought as he fell back onto his bed and looked at the ceiling. Then he remembered when he was smaller and his parents prayed with him at bedtime. They used a little poem, and part of it said: "And if I die before I wake, I pray the Lord my soul to take."

If I died tonight . . .

Jimmy didn't like it. And suddenly he didn't like Dave or Jacob or the way they had tricked him into going to church that night. *What kind of maniac would give a kid my age a booklet that talks about dying? They must be warped*, Jimmy concluded.

Once again, he set his mind to coming up with a scheme to get out of going to church.

CHAPTER FIVE

Saturday Night

J immy failed to devise an escape. Dave and Jacob picked him up right on time. *They want to be absolutely sure I make it*, he figured.

The club meeting started 10 minutes late in what everyone at the church called the "fellowship hall." It was a large, auditoriumlike room just off the main sanctuary. Jimmy knew it from the Sunday school assembly his parents made him attend every week. It had multiple purposes, with a marked floor for sports games and enough blackboards and wall space to work for teaching. With the addition of a few long tables, it also served as a banquet hall for events like Valentine's Day or Back-to-School or End-of-School get-togethers, depending on the time of year.

Because he'd never paid much attention on Sunday

mornings to know who attended, Jimmy was surprised by some of the faces he recognized. Many of the most popular kids from school were there. Kids of all ages showed up. Jimmy dropped himself onto a folding chair along the wall and figured that those kids were there because somebody *made them* go—just like him.

Jack Davis, who was in the same grade as Jimmy, sat down next to him. "Hey, Jimmy, what're you doing here?" he asked.

"I don't know," Jimmy said with a shrug. "I got tricked into coming. What are *you* doing here?"

"I come every week."

"Really? Your parents make you?"

"At first they did, but now I come because I want to. It's a lot of fun," Jack said. "There's Lucy and Oscar! I'll see you later." And Jack took off to greet his friends.

Jimmy was surprised. Jack's answer wasn't what he would have expected. As he looked more closely at the expressions on the faces of the kids mingling around, saying hi to one another or talking about how they had spent their Saturdays, he realized they didn't seem dejected like him. They didn't look as if they minded being there at all.

Jacob walked in, saw Jimmy, and waved. Jimmy nodded. Jacob looked as if he might come over but was distracted by his dad whistling through his fingers to get everyone's attention.

As they quieted down and took their seats, Dave took hold of a microphone attached to a portable podium. He welcomed one and all in a voice made thin by the cheap speaker. He asked any visitors to stand up and say their names, and a couple of kids scattered through the crowd complied. Jimmy didn't. Dave realized it and, not to be undone, announced that Jimmy was there. Jimmy blushed and leaned forward, resting his arms on his knees, wishing he'd never agreed to that stupid basketball game. He didn't belong here. He didn't belong with any of these people. He belonged with Tony somewhere at Allen's Pond, spying on Tony's older brother. But it was too late now. All he could do was hope the evening would slip by as quickly as possible.

Dave introduced a guest speaker, Mr. Lucas, one of the church's deacons. Jimmy recognized him from the times he got up to pray in the services.

Mr. Lucas talked for almost 15 minutes, and about halfway through, Jimmy realized he was having a hard time understanding a word the man was saying. A couple of times he mentioned having an abundant life and calling on some sort of power and being born again by being washed in the blood of the Lamb for remission of something or other and inheriting some kind of eternal thingy in a kingdom of a lot of big words in a fullness of time affixed before Adam fell in his garden and . . .

Jimmy felt as if he were drowning in a sea of weird words. He had a vague idea of what Mr. Lucas was trying to say, and Mr. Lucas was obviously sincere, but Jimmy got so lost that he could only stare at the pattern of marking tape on the floor.

Mr. Lucas finished his talk on a loud and excited note and

stepped away. Dave took the podium again and announced that it was time to split up into various grades for games. Jimmy was relieved to find himself in a game of dodgeball with Jacob, Jack, Lucy, Oscar, and a few other kids he knew from school. He was especially proud when he held out the longest and was the last one in the circle to get hit.

Then they played a bean-bag toss, ran a relay race, and played a game Jimmy had never seen before where they lay down on their backs and kicked an enormous ball from one side of the room to another. The idea was to score by hitting the other team's wall. Jimmy alternately screamed and laughed through all the games. Time slipped away. He was shocked when they stopped for snacks and drinks and he realized it was after nine o'clock.

All the kids gathered again for a few final words from Dave. Jimmy braced himself for another sermon with a lot of words and expressions he didn't understand.

Dave spoke simply, however. "I can't let any of you out of here tonight without making a few things absolutely clear," he said. "We try to have a lot of fun when we meet like this, but we're not here just for fun. We're here to get to know each other. We're here to have fellowship with other Christians. And we're here to see that there are ways to enjoy ourselves without doing what a lot of our friends think is fun—the kinds of things that get us in trouble, that lead nowhere and don't give you anything except a few seconds of pleasure."

Dave held up a booklet just like the one he gave Jimmy

earlier that day. "I've handed out this booklet to a lot of you over the last few days. I'll bet most of you haven't read it. You looked at the front and said, 'Hey, I'm just a kid. What do I care about dying?'"

Jimmy squirmed in his chair and wondered how Dave knew that.

"I understand how you feel," Dave continued. "You don't care about the past or the future. All you care about is *right now*—what games you play, what's on television, what kind of music is really hot, what all the other kids are doing. Today is all there is for you. Living for the great big *right now*. You're too young to feel you have a past. You're too young to feel there's really a future. And if there *is* a future out there for you, dying isn't part of it. So why did I give you these booklets?"

Good question, Jimmy thought.

Dave laughed and said, "I gave you these booklets because we have two boxes of them in the church office and we didn't know what else to do with them."

Some of the kids snickered.

Dave's laugh tapered off. "Actually," he said, "I gave them to you because of what they say inside. Did any of you read what was on the inside?"

Jimmy glanced around, but no one raised a hand.

Dave went on. "See, these booklets are supposed to make you *think*, if only for a minute. Any of us could die at any time. Any of us could die *right now*. The same *right now* that you live in day after day. I'm not trying to scare you. I'm just saying there's something *more* to this world than we realize. There's a lot more to it than games, television, music, what the other kids are doing, finishing your homework, or eating all the right vegetables. In fact, there's a whole *other* world. An eternal one. One that goes on forever. And it's not some kind of comic-book place. It's *God's* place. It's *real*. And it's even more real than *this* world."

Dave knocked on the podium as if to say that the "this world" he was talking about was the one that could be rapped with your knuckles. It was the world Jimmy could see with his two eyes and touch with his two hands.

It made Jimmy sit up. He stared at Dave and wished he *could* see the other world or touch it somehow. Maybe that would make a difference. Maybe then Jimmy could . . .

Could what? he wondered. *Could what?*

"But y'know," Dave said with a smile, "when I was your age, I figured there was no point in thinking about any other worlds, because I have to live in this one. None of us can be Alice slipping through the looking glass or Peter stepping through the closet into Narnia or a captain on the Enterprise warping to another galaxy. We're stuck *here* for now. And that's why God had to do something radical. God had to make a move. Do you know what He did?"

Jimmy waited for the answer.

"God stepped into *our* world. He put on skin and hair and muscles and clothes and became just like *us*. He took on a name—Jesus. He did it so we could have some of that other world in *our* world. He did it so we could go to that other world and be with Him when the time is right. But it wasn't easy for Him. It cost Him *a lot* to do it. I know some of you guys know what I'm talking about."

Jimmy knew, but he wanted to hear Dave say it anyway.

Dave said, "That other world is a perfect place, just as God is perfect. But we're not. No matter what we do, we can't be good enough to go there. So God had to do something even *more* radical than just walk around in our world. He had to come up with a way to get us imperfect people into His perfect world. And the only way to do that was to die—for you and me and all our imperfections—our *sins*—and He did it in the most painful way possible: on a cross. He did it because we couldn't do it for ourselves. I can't do enough or be good enough. You can't, either. No matter what you try to do to make yourself better, it won't be good enough. Do you understand? He *had to do it*—and He did it *for you*."

Those words hung in the air, and for a moment Jimmy felt as though it were just him and Dave in the room. *He had to do it, and He did it for me*, Jimmy thought.

"But dying wasn't enough," Dave continued. "Anybody can die and be put in a grave to rot. Nothing special about that. But Jesus died and then came out of the grave. Death couldn't hold Him down. He rose up so that we could rise up, too. And when we rise up, we rise to that other place, the place where God lives. And we'll live with Him. But until then . . ."

Dave shoved his hands into his pockets and moved away

from the pulpit. He walked into the crowd of kids sitting on chairs and on the floor and spoke as if to each one. "What's the catch? you're wondering. He did all that for me, but what's He want in return? Well, I'll tell you . . ."

Jimmy held on to his chair. Dave was now in the middle of the crowd.

"He wants your *life*," Dave said in a harsh whisper. "He wants every bit of you: your heart, your mind, your body, your *soul*. And He doesn't want it so He can lock it away somewhere and make you a miserable, boring religious person from now on. He wants it so He can work on it, turn it into something new . . . and then give it back to you in better shape than it was before."

Dave turned and scanned the crowd before he spoke again.

"Maybe you think you're too young—this is stuff for grown-ups. It isn't. Even if dying is years and years away for you, the decision to believe in Jesus, to accept Him into your hearts and give Him your lives, begins *right now*." Dave looked Jimmy square in the eyes. "Jesus wants you *right now*."

CHAPTER SIX

Late Saturday Night

J immy was surprised by how he felt as the meeting ended.
Somehow it had never struck him that Jesus might
actually *want* him or that Jesus died *for him*. Yeah, he'd
heard those things in Sunday school and church. But for some
reason it hadn't hit him until now that Jesus' death and res-
urrection demanded that he do something in return. Until now,
Jesus was always something he could pick or not pick—like an
answer on a multiple-choice test. But here He was . . . wanting
Jimmy *right now*.

Jimmy thought about it as Dave and Jacob give him a lift
home. Jimmy hoped Dave wouldn't say anything to him or
ask him any questions. He was afraid an additional word or
question might spoil the whole thing. Maybe they sensed it,
too, because neither of them spoke. They drove in silence

except for an exchange of "Good night" when Jimmy got out of the car and walked to his front door.

He died for me. . . . He wants me. . . . He wants every bit of me. My heart, my mind, my body, my soul. And He doesn't want it so He can lock it away somewhere and make me a miserable, boring religious person from now on. He wants it so He can work on it, turn it into something new . . . and then give it back to me in better shape than it was before.

Jimmy drifted past the living room. His mom called out from her reading chair. Jimmy peeked in.

"How was it?" she asked.

Jimmy shrugged and said, "Okay, I guess."

"Not as bad as you thought?"

"I guess not," he answered. "A bunch of kids I know were there. We played some games and stuff. It was okay."

Mary smiled. "Good," she said. "Now do me a favor and go have a bath."

"A bath!"

"Uh huh. We have church tomorrow, and after tonight's exercise, I'm sure you need one. Go on," she insisted.

"Okay," Jimmy said and went up the stairs.

Donna came out of the bathroom just as he reached the door. "What happened to you?" she asked.

"What do you mean?" Jimmy said.

"You look like something's wrong."

"I'm gonna have a bath," he answered.

"Oh. That must be it." She giggled and strode to her room.

Jimmy went into the bathroom, turned on the water, and stripped down. He thought about God putting on skin, hair, and muscles so He could be like us . . . so He could die like us . . . for us. *For me.*

The words wouldn't leave Jimmy alone. They were like rubber bands, so that no matter what his mind wandered to in the warm cocoon of the bathwater, it snapped back to those words. *For me. And He wants me right now.*

Jimmy absentmindedly scrubbed himself, then pulled the plug at the bottom of the tub. The water gurgled and gulped. He stepped out of the tub. *What if I said yes?* he wondered as he dried himself off. *What would happen if I said He could have me right now?*

His heart beat a little faster at the thought. Would angels sing? Would he hear God whisper in his ear? Would lightning strike the house? What would happen?

Jimmy wrapped the towel around himself, strolled toward his room—got halfway there when he remembered he had left his clothes on the bathroom floor and went back to get them—then resumed his journey. *Jesus wants me right now. What if I say yes?*

Say yes.

In his room, Jimmy looked around for the small, black Bible his grandmother had given him for his birthday a couple of years before. It had his name in gold letters at the bottom of the front cover. What had he done with it? He got down on his hands and knees to look under the bed. Was that it in the far corner? He got up and rounded the bed, kneeling once again to get the Bible. But it wasn't there. Nothing was there. *It must've been a shadow*, Jimmy thought.

He stayed on his knees. Quietly, without fanfare or announcement, the yes slipped from his head to his heart. It happened in the fraction of a second while Donna's muffled radio played on the other side of the wall, his mother coughed once downstairs in the living room, and the night was otherwise silent enough for him to hear the pounding in his chest and the blood rushing past his ears. *Yes.* He pressed his head against the side of the bed. *You died for me, and I'm sorry, and now You want me—all of me—and I'm saying yes.*

Jimmy opened his eyes and stood up. That was that. It was done. He looked around, but there was no flash of lightning, no supernatural appearance, no voices. He didn't even feel any different. It didn't matter. He wasn't disappointed. He had said yes.

He went downstairs and didn't say a word about it to his mom. Instead, he talked her into letting him have a small glass of chocolate milk before he went to bed.

It seemed so simple. And as he went to sleep, he thought about how everything would get better. Jesus would take his life, fix it up, and hand it back. All Jimmy had to do was watch it happen.

Jimmy had no idea what he'd gotten himself into.

CHAPTER SEVEN

Sunday Morning

With bleary eyes, fluffy bathrobe, and worn slippers, Mary Barclay walked into the kitchen to make coffee. She yawned as she passed the kitchen table where Jimmy sat. She nodded at him and turned to plug in the coffeemaker. Her hand, holding the plug, stopped in midair as the vision of what she had just seen registered on her sleepy brain. She swung on her heel to face the table again.

Jimmy sat at the table in his church outfit—washed and ready to go.

Mary's mouth fell open.

Donna walked into the kitchen in the same state of early morning disrepair as her mother and also gasped when she saw Jimmy. "You . . . you're up," Donna said.

"Uh huh," Jimmy said.

"You're dressed and ready to go to church," Jimmy's mom said.

"Uh huh," Jimmy said.

"Are you feeling all right?" Donna asked. Then she turned to her mother and asked, "Does he have a fever?"

"I don't think so," Mary replied. "Do you have a fever, Jimmy?"

"No," Jimmy said.

"He doesn't have a fever," Mary told Donna.

"Then what's wrong with him?" Donna asked.

"I don't know," Mary said, then looked at Jimmy. "What's wrong with you?"

Jimmy smiled and said, "What makes you think something's wrong?"

"Because we usually have to drag you out of bed kicking and screaming to go to church, that's what," Donna said.

"Really? That's terrible. I'll have to work on that," Jimmy said. "Mom? Are you gonna plug in the coffeemaker or stand there with it in your hand for the rest of the morning?"

Mary looked at the plug in her hand, then turned to plug it in.

"Okay, what's going on?" Donna demanded with her hands on her hips.

"If you hang around asking me questions, we're all gonna be late for church," Jimmy said.

"But—"

"He's right, Donna," Mary interrupted. "I don't want to spoil whatever's gotten into him by asking a lot of questions.

Let's just . . . make the most of it."

The routine to get ready for church continued as usual—except that this time Jimmy was the one waiting for everyone else. He didn't tell them what had happened the night before. Not yet. He wanted to relish their surprise and curiosity at his mysterious behavior.

*****

Jimmy walked to his Sunday school class as if it were his first time there. Rather than drag himself down the hall with a scowl on his face as he normally did, he walked quickly, taking in all the sights with a nervous anticipation. *What* he anticipated, he didn't know. But it was the first Sunday he was in church after he had said yes, and everything seemed new to him. He felt as if it were the first day of school. He felt like a stranger, even though he'd been there week after week since he was seven years old. He felt that way not because no one knew him, but because he didn't really know them. All the kids moving to and from their Sunday school classes from various assemblies, clutching their Bibles and lesson books, looked as if he'd never seen them before. No longer were they Sunday school zombies as he had always thought of them. Now—*now* they were alive because Jimmy was alive. And he was alive because he had said yes.

Jimmy's wide-eyed reverie was suddenly interrupted by someone grabbing his arm. "Whoa! Where're you going in such a hurry?" Dave Wright asked.

Jimmy was too startled to answer right away.

Dave took a step back and looked him over. "Something's happened," he said. "You look different. This isn't the frowning, I-don't-want-to-be-here Jimmy Barclay I'm used to seeing on Sundays. What's going on?"

Jimmy smiled awkwardly. His heart picked up a few beats as he tried to say the words. If anybody should hear first, it was Dave. But how could he say it?

"Well?"

Jimmy swallowed hard. "I . . . I said yes."

"Yes?" Dave looked puzzled.

Jimmy nodded. "You said Jesus wanted me, and I said yes—He can have me."

Dave's face instantly lit up. "Jimmy! Are you serious? You really accepted Jesus?"

Jimmy smiled and said, "Yeah!"

"Yahoo!" Dave shouted, scooping Jimmy up in his arms. It wasn't what Jimmy expected, and he was a little embarrassed when everyone in the hall stopped to look. "Praise God!"

"Hey! Cut it out!" Jimmy said.

Dave put Jimmy down. "Jimmy, that's *wonderful!* Wonderful!" And he grabbed Jimmy again for a bone-crushing hug.

"Lay off!" Jimmy said.

"Sorry." Dave let him go. "I'm a tactile person."

"I hope it isn't catching."

"It means I'm a huggy kind of person," Dave said with a laugh.

"I hope that isn't catching either," Jimmy said.

A bell rang.

"We're late for Sunday school," Dave said, moving away. "You go on and I'll . . . invite myself over to your house for Sunday dinner or something so we can talk about it. See you in church!" He gave Jimmy a thumbs-up and smiled before he disappeared down the hall.

*****

Just like Sunday school, the church service took on a whole new meaning for Jimmy. The hymns, the Bible readings, and the prayers all seemed created just for him. The pastor's sermon still made him fidget and want to doodle on the offering envelopes, but besides that, he *liked* it. For the first time, he *really liked it*.

During the final hymn, Jimmy leaned over to his mother. "Mom?"

She continued to sing while she leaned her ear toward Jimmy.

"Mom," Jimmy began. He wanted to say it just right, so he used the phrase Dave used earlier. "I accepted Jesus last night."

Mary sang another few words, then the hymnbook in her hand slumped a little. She closed her eyes for a moment. When she opened them again to look at Jimmy, they were tear-filled. She pulled him close with her free hand. It wasn't enough. She laid the hymnbook on the pew and embraced him long and hard with both arms. Jimmy wasn't as embarrassed as he was with Dave. This hug was all right.

From the corner of his eye, he saw Donna stare at them as if they'd lost their minds.

CHAPTER EIGHT

Sunday Afternoon

Dave, his wife, Jan, and Jacob invited themselves to a Sunday meal at the Barclays'. Mary said there was plenty of food to go around and she'd love to have them. She wished George would get home from his mother's in time, she added, but she didn't know when he'd make it. Besides that, it seemed like a perfect way to celebrate Jimmy's decision.

Jimmy wasn't sure if the dinner felt more as if it were his birthday or Thanksgiving. Either way, it felt like a special occasion. Jacob was as quiet as always, while Dave entertained them all with stories of other churches where he had been a kids' minister. Jimmy thought Jan was rather quiet but really pretty. Now that he saw her up close, he realized Jacob looked more like her than Dave.

After dinner, Jacob gently smiled and gave Jimmy a small box. Jimmy opened it to find a new Bible.

"We didn't know if you already had one," Dave said, "but I figured some of the study helps in there might be good for you."

"Thanks," Jimmy said and flipped open the cover. On the inside was written: "To Jimmy Barclay, for saying yes to life's greatest adventure . . . with Jesus! Love, Dave, Jan, and Jacob."

After they all helped to clear away the dishes, Dave took Jimmy into the living room and sat him down. "How do you feel?" Dave asked.

Jimmy shrugged. "I don't know," he said. "How am I supposed to feel?"

"It's hard to say. Some people feel like crying, some feel like laughing, and some don't feel anything at all."

"I guess I feel funny about all this fuss," Jimmy said.

"I would, too," Dave said, "but I brought you in here to talk about some things you should know."

"Like what?"

"Well . . ." Dave paused as if trying to choose his words carefully. "Being a Christian isn't like anything you've experienced before. You and Jesus are directly connected now because His Spirit is living inside you. That means things are going to change for you."

"Change? Like how?"

"For one thing, you're going to grow as a Christian. That means you'll develop and mature in the faith. And that growth is just like any other growth. Sometimes it happens in spurts, and other times it happens so slowly you hardly notice."

"Okay," Jimmy said, wondering when his growth would start to happen.

Dave said, "It takes work, Jimmy. The Spirit doesn't just take over and automatically do things. You have to read your Bible every day and obey what it says. You'll want to pray as much as you can. You'll need to spend time with other Christians at church. And you'll want to tell others about your faith. It's a great adventure, Jimmy, it really is."

Jimmy smiled. He liked adventures—especially adventures that changed things for the better.

Dave leaned forward and said quietly, "But make no mistake, Jimmy. It's an adventure that can be difficult and painful sometimes. You'll see."

Jimmy looked at Dave uneasily. That didn't seem like a very nice thing to say.

The front storm door banged, and the inside door opened. George Barclay stepped through, clumsily lugging his overnight bag. "Oh, hi," he said with a weary smile. "I didn't know we were having a party. Hi, Dave."

"We figured we'd take over while you were gone," Dave said.

"Hey, Dad!" Jimmy called out. "You'll never guess what happened!"

"Yeah, you wouldn't believe it in a million years," Donna said as she emerged from the other room with Mary, Jan, and Jacob.

"Why? What happened?" George asked. He dropped his bag, and Mary kissed him hello. Then he waved hello to Jan and Jacob.

"Go on, tell him," Mary instructed Jimmy.

"I accepted Jesus last night," Jimmy said.

George looked from Jimmy to Mary and back again. "You did?"

"Uh huh," Jimmy said.

"Jimmy . . . Jimmy . . ." George simply said his name over and over as he moved across the room toward him. He pulled Jimmy close for a hug. "Son . . . I don't know what to say."

"Just say you're glad," Jimmy answered.

George whispered, "I'm glad, son. I'm so glad." Suddenly he held Jimmy at arm's length. "Wait a minute. This isn't a trick to get out of being punished for that stunt you pulled the other night?"

"No, Dad," Jimmy said and rolled his eyes.

George laughed and pulled Jimmy back for another hug. "Good."

*****

Everyone gathered in the living room for coffee and soft drinks while George reluctantly reported that his mother's health was going downhill. Even with treatment, the cancer was ravaging her body. The doctors couldn't guess how long she had to live.

Jimmy sat silently while his dad spoke. He was a Christian now, and his grandmother was going to die. It didn't seem right somehow.

Dave suggested they take a minute to pray for her, so they did. Jimmy was horrified when Dave asked him to start.

"Me?"

Dave nodded.

"Out loud?"

"Yes, please."

"But I don't know how," Jimmy said.

"Just do it like you've heard it in church," his dad suggested. "You can do it."

Jimmy looked on helplessly as everyone bowed his or her head and waited. Finally, he started: "Um . . . heavenly Father . . . uh, we thank Thee for the things which Thou has, uh, spoken to our faces, and, uh, we pray that as we disregard the things we know today that, uh, You will be ever-pressured, uh, while we, uh, remain mindless of You. . . ."

Donna snickered.

Jimmy told her to shut up.

George put his hand on Jimmy's arm. "Son, just pray what's on your heart, okay? Just pray for Grandma."

Jimmy nodded and bowed his head again. "Dear God, please make Grandma better. Amen."

"Amen," everyone echoed.

Then Dave prayed long and hard for Jimmy's grandma, saying all the things Jimmy's heart had wanted him to say without knowing how.

CHAPTER NINE

Late Sunday Afternoon and Evening

The Wright family went home late in the afternoon, but not before confirming that Jimmy would go to the evening church service. They wanted him to go forward at the closing altar call to present himself as a candidate for baptism. Jimmy wasn't keen about going forward in front of all those people. Dave assured him it was nothing to be embarrassed about. It was the next step of obedience in his yes to Jesus. Jimmy reluctantly agreed.

In the silence of his room, he decided to read his new Bible. He figured the best thing was to start at Genesis 1:1 and read through the whole Bible.

He was asleep before he got to Genesis 2:3.

Amidst dreams of firmaments, ocean waves, and blinding light, a gentle knocking woke him up. It was Tony at the window again. Jimmy threw it open.

"Hey, Jimmy," Tony said. "What're you doing?"

"Do you have a death wish or something? Why do you keep coming to my window?" Jimmy responded.

"Because your parents won't let me come to the front door," he said. "Don't you wanna hear about last night?"

"Last night?"

"Allen's Pond! Me and Brad Woodward followed my brother and his friends up to the barbecue area on top of the hill. They took booze and everything! You should've seen them!"

"Did they catch you this time?"

Tony shook his head. "Nope. This time we hid around by the utility shack. Dale Miller walked right up to us to throw a bottle away and didn't even see us!"

Jimmy wished he could've been there.

"You really missed it," Tony said. "That's what you get for going to that stupid church meeting."

"It wasn't stupid," Jimmy said defensively.

"Oh, really?"

"Yeah, it was . . . good." Jimmy felt a hot rush of embarrassment. He didn't know what to say to Tony, how to tell him what had happened.

"What was so good about it?"

"I . . . well, we played a lot of games and stuff," Jimmy said. "And then . . . then . . . I came home."

"Sounds like a blast," Tony said sarcastically.

"Something happened. . . . "

"Like what?"

Jimmy's eyes darted around the room nervously. He didn't dare look Tony in the face or he'd lose his nerve. How could he tell Tony he'd become a Christian when he and Tony used to laugh at them?

"This branch is hurting my arm. I gotta go," Tony said when it didn't look as though Jimmy would answer his question.

"Wait," Jimmy said, then blurted out, "I became a Christian last night."

Tony laughed. "You did what?" he said.

"I became a Christian," Jimmy repeated.

"Cool!" Tony said. "What a great idea!"

For the first time, Jimmy looked him in the eyes. "What?" he asked, surprised.

"It's a great way to get your parents off your back! Hey, maybe they'll take you off restriction!" Tony said.

Jimmy frowned. "That's not why I did it!"

Tony smiled as if to say, "I don't believe a word you're saying."

"I'm serious, Tony," Jimmy said. "See, Dave talked about how Jesus died for us and . . . how He wants me and . . . and . . . I said yes. I'm even going back tonight to tell the church I want to be baptized."

It sounded so ridiculous to Jimmy's ears, he could imagine what Tony must've been thinking.

"You're lying to me," Tony said.

"Huh uh," Jimmy answered.

Tony renewed his grip on the tree branch. "I don't get it, Jimmy. Did they brainwash you or what? You're tellin' me you're turning into a Chip Bender or something?"

Chip Bender was a former friend of theirs who became a Christian and talked about Jesus all the time after that. It drove everybody at school nuts.

"No!" Jimmy said, then added, "I mean, I don't know. It just happened!"

"Oh, man," Tony said, shaking his head. "This isn't good."

"What's wrong?"

"You're gonna become a monk and preach to the raccoons in the woods. I just know it," he said.

"I am not!" Jimmy protested.

From downstairs, Jimmy's mom called that it was time to go to church.

"You'd better go to *church* now, Jimmy," Tony said and began to back away on the branch. "You don't wanna miss your chance to preach."

"Cut it out!" Jimmy said.

"See ya, Mr. Sunday School," Tony said before he disappeared at the bottom of the tree.

"I don't care what you say," Jimmy shouted after him.

Some friend Tony turned out to be, he thought as he closed the window. But, of course, Jimmy *did* care what Tony thought. He cared a lot.

*****

Jimmy brooded on Tony all during the church service. At first, he worried that he'd lost his best friend. Then he got angry about Tony's teasing. Then he wondered if he had made a big mistake in saying yes to Jesus. Would he become Mr. Sunday School? Then he got mad again because Tony spoiled the night he was going forward for baptism.

The pastor finished preaching, and everyone stood to sing the closing hymn—the *invitation*, it was called. George Barclay put his hand on Jimmy's shoulder and leaned close to his ear. "I know it's a little embarrassing," he said. "Will you let me go up with you?"

Jimmy smiled as thoughts of Tony disappeared instantly. "Yeah," he said.

George kept his arm across Jimmy's shoulders as they stepped into the aisle and walked to the front of the church. Jimmy was vaguely aware of the rows of people on both sides, but they were merely trees in a human forest.

The pastor greeted them with a big smile. "Hi, George. Hello, Jimmy," he said.

George cleared his throat and said, "Jimmy accepted Jesus last night and would like to be baptized."

"Congratulations!" the pastor said warmly. He then looked at George expectantly, as if there were something else to be said.

Jimmy looked up at his dad's face and suddenly realized tears were rolling down his cheeks.

"Because my son accepted Jesus, I want to rededicate my

life to Christ," George said and squeezed Jimmy's shoulder.

"Me, too," came a tear-filled voice from behind Jimmy. He turned. It was his mother.

"So do I," came a younger choked-up voice. It was Donna.

As the organ played softly, the Barclay family collected themselves into a tender embrace. And Jimmy found himself crying, too.

CHAPTER TEN

Monday at School

Jimmy set his radio alarm clock for Q96—Odyssey's only Christian station. He thought he would wake up to music. Instead, he awakened to a fiery preacher who was making a case about lazy Christians who never talked about Jesus to their families, friends, and neighbors. He made his point by citing Acts chapter 2. "Look what happened here," the preacher said. "After the Holy Spirit descended upon the disciples, Peter went out into the street to preach the story of Jesus. At first, the people thought the disciples were drunk because they were so filled with the power of the Spirit. Peter set them straight. He said, 'Hey, you heathens, we're not drunk! We're just fulfilling what the prophet Joel said would happen! He said that in the last days, young men and women would prophesy and see visions and dream dreams! And that's exactly what's happening right here, right now!'"

Jimmy rolled over in his bed and listened.

"Then Peter went on and laid the gospel down for everyone who was listening. He told them about how God sent Jesus of Nazareth to them, and they crucified Him because their hearts were hard, but it didn't matter because Jesus rose from the dead to prove He's their Lord and Messiah! And look at what the people did.

"The people said, 'What're we supposed to do?' and Peter told them to repent and be baptized in the name of Jesus the Messiah, and then their sins would be forgiven.

"You see what he did? He told them the gospel, plain and simple, and they responded. He *witnessed* to them.

"Do you know what witnessing is? Witnessing is telling what you know. Like if you saw a car accident, you'd act as a *witness*—you'd tell the police and the court what you saw, what you know. That's what Peter did. He told them what he knew. And they responded by asking how they could know Jesus the way Peter did. And look at verse 41. Do you see that verse? *Three thousand* people were added to the church that day! *Three thousand*—all because Peter took the time to share the gospel. He could've made all the excuses we make—about how we're tired or embarrassed or don't want to be pushy. Did Peter care? No! He obeyed Scripture, called on the power of the Holy Spirit, and explained his faith, and *three thousand* became believers."

Someone knocked on Jimmy's bedroom door.

"Yeah?" Jimmy called out.

"Just making sure you're up," his mother said. "We don't want you to be late for school."

"Okay," Jimmy said and sat up. The preacher had finished speaking, and an announcer was telling about booklets listeners could order. Jimmy turned off the radio and got ready for school.

It would be his first day there as a new Christian, and he wanted to make it count. If Peter could bring three thousand people to their knees, Jimmy could at least do the same with a couple of kids. One way or another, he was going to make an impact.

And he did.

*****

The morning at school slipped past in a blur of history, English, and math. Jimmy and Tony were in different classes, so he didn't get to see him until lunch. Tony was sitting with Brad Woodward when Jimmy walked up to their table.

"Hey, Tony," Jimmy said as he sat down.

Tony and Brad stopped their conversation to look at Jimmy. "What's up, Jimmy?" Tony said.

"Not much," Jimmy said. That was one of their normal exchanges, like when adults say "Hi, how are you?" and the other says "Fine" even if he isn't fine.

"Brad and I were just talking about Saturday night at Allen's Pond," Tony explained. Then he said to Brad, "Jimmy couldn't go with us 'cause he was in trouble and had to go to church. Right, Jimmy?"

Jimmy answered, "Yeah, well, I—"

Tony continued saying to Brad, "Did I tell you that Jimmy's all religious now? He's gonna grow up and be one of those TV evangelist guys." Tony and Brad laughed.

"Cut it out, Tony! I am not," Jimmy said.

"He'll have to paint his hair white and get sweaty and talk in a REAL LOUD VOICE," Brad added.

"He'll have to buy a white suit," Tony said with a laugh.

Jimmy wondered if Peter had to put up with this kind of junk. "Don't be morons," Jimmy said.

"I still think you're just pulling something to get out of trouble with your parents," Tony said.

"No, I'm not," Jimmy said.

"Then come on, tell us what happened," Tony said.

Jimmy thought back to what the preacher had said that morning: Witnessing is just telling what happened, and then *three thousand* could be saved. So Jimmy sent up a quick prayer for the Holy Spirit to help him make Tony and Brad fall to their knees and become Christians right there. He began, "See, I went to church the other night, and I thought it'd be really boring, but it wasn't. We played games, and then Dave, one of our pastors, talked and said that—"

"What kind of games?" Brad asked.

"I don't know," Jimmy answered impatiently, "dodgeball and stuff. Shut up and listen, will you? Anyway, Dave told us how we all live in this world, but there's another world that God lives in, and so God sent Jesus to *this* world to—"

"So Jesus was some kind of astronaut," Tony teased. "A UFO."

"No," Jimmy said. "But, see, He came over and dressed in skin and stuff so He could be like us."

Brad raised his hand as if he were asking a question in class. "How did He put on the skin?" he asked. "Did it have a zipper up the back, like the monster in *Creature from the Black Lagoon?*" He and Tony laughed again.

Annoyed, Jimmy folded his arms. "He was *born*, you idiots! Don't you know what Christmas is all about?"

Tony smiled and said, "It's about a big tree and presents and Santa Claus."

"Maybe Santa Claus was Jesus in disguise," Brad said with a chuckle.

"Will you quit fooling around?" Jimmy pleaded. "Do you wanna know what happened or not?"

"Yeah, but skip the history lesson," Tony said.

"It's not a history lesson, it's part of the story," Jimmy said. "You have to understand why He came! See, we're no good, and God is perfect, so Jesus had to come and die so that we could be with God. We can't go to the other place unless we're made perfect, kinda like Jesus is and ... and ..."

Tony's and Brad's blank expressions told Jimmy he wasn't making any sense at all. Why couldn't he say it the way Dave did? Why couldn't he sound like Peter? Why were Tony and

Brad giggling? *I'll bet Peter's audience didn't giggle*, he thought.

Tony burst out laughing. "I wish you could see your face!" he said. "You don't even know what you're talking about!"

Tony and Brad laughed harder, then harder still.

"I do, too! You just don't understand!" Jimmy protested.

They kept laughing and making more jokes about Santa Claus, aliens, other worlds, and everything else Jimmy had tried to say.

It wasn't supposed to happen this way, he thought as his emotions twisted up and nearly squeezed tears out of him. *They're supposed to understand and say yes to Jesus just like me. Why don't they?*

Finally, he grabbed his tray of food and stormed off to another table.

Jack, Oscar, and Lucy were sitting together as Jimmy passed their table. Jack called out, but Jimmy ignored him. He wanted to ignore everyone. He couldn't stand the thought of being laughed at any more.

CHAPTER ELEVEN

Monday After School

After school, Jimmy avoided Tony and went straight home. He was still moping about what had happened at lunch, but in case he was asked, he had worked out an excuse about rushing home to finish building a model of a ship. His dad had given him the model two Christmases ago, and it was still unassembled in a box at the top of his closet, but Jimmy ran home anyway.

It nagged at Jimmy that he had prayed for the Holy Spirit to help him—just like Peter—and they had laughed at him anyway. He couldn't understand why they didn't want to say yes to Jesus the same way he had after hearing Dave.

In his room, he paced and tried to figure it out. He wished— no, it was really a prayer, though Jimmy didn't realize it—that he could talk to somebody who understood how he felt. At that moment, he thought he was the only person in the world who had ever become a new Christian and was teased about it.

His mind went back to the ship model, so he climbed up on a chair to pull it down. As he pushed and lifted various games and boxes of long-forgotten toys, something caught his eye in the corner of the shelf. It was the Bible his grandmother had given him—the one with his name embossed on the front cover. He grabbed it, climbed off the chair, and threw himself onto his bed. Dust blew from the book's jacket. The binding cracked as he opened it. On the inside, his grandmother had written:

> For Jimmy,
>
> Do not let people look down on you because you are young, but be to them an example in your speech and behavior, in your love and faith and sincerity. (1 Tim. 4:12)
>
> Love, Grandma B.

Was this the answer to his wish-that-was-really-a-prayer? "Don't let people look down on you," it said. "Be an example in your speech and behavior." Is that what God wanted him to know? He couldn't be sure.

Then Jimmy thought about his grandmother. He suddenly felt a longing to talk to her, to see her. She had always acted as though Jimmy would become a Christian one day, and now that he had, he wanted to make sure she knew about it. Had his dad told her? Would they let him call her? Maybe he could go and visit. He wanted to do *something*.

He remembered once again how his family used to pray together. He wondered how it would feel now to pray—and really mean it. He closed the Bible and crawled off his bed. Getting on his knees next to it, he carefully folded his hands and began, "Dear God—"

Just then, Donna walked into the room. "Jimmy," she said.

Jimmy instantly fell to the floor and pretended he was searching for something under his bed. "What?" he shouted. "Don't you ever knock?"

"Sorry!" she said. "What're you doing?"

"I'm looking for something!" he said, still talking loudly from his embarrassment.

Donna looked puzzled. "Oh," she responded. "Well, Jacob's here to see you."

"Jacob Wright?" Jimmy asked as he stood up.

"How many other Jacobs do you know?" Donna said as she walked out. Jimmy heard her call down the stairs for Jacob to come up.

Jimmy was surprised. He couldn't imagine that Jacob would show up without his father. He wondered what he was doing there. He also wondered what he would have to talk about with a kid who never seemed to talk.

Jacob peeked into the room. "Hi," he said softly.

"Hi," Jimmy said.

"I heard you had a hard time today," Jacob said.

Jimmy knew that Jacob was taught at home by his mom, so he didn't go to their school. "How did you hear about it?"

"My dad saw Jack Davis at Whit's End, and he said your friends were teasing you at lunch. You tried to witness to them, huh? They didn't act the way you thought they would."

Jimmy stared at Jacob for a moment. "They're idiots," he finally said, and all the feelings from lunch came rushing back to him. He felt angry and wanted to cry.

"They don't get it," Jacob said quietly as he sat on the edge of the bed. "Maybe they'll *never* get it. That's the way it happens sometimes. They all make up their own minds. All you can do is what God says to do and *try* to tell them."

"But Tony's my best friend! He was supposed to . . . to understand." Jimmy hung his head. "I said it all wrong."

Jacob smiled. "Just because you became a Christian doesn't mean you'll turn into Peter or Paul and be a great preacher right away," he said. "I know. The same thing happened to me the first time I tried to tell someone about Jesus."

"Really?" Jimmy asked, brightening a little.

"Yeah," Jacob confirmed. "I felt embarrassed and mad, and . . . I thought I might cry in front of everybody. It was terrible."

Jimmy sat down on his bed next to Jacob. He looked intently at the brown-haired kid who didn't talk much but came by at just the right time as if he had been sent by someone.

Jimmy realized he wasn't alone after all. His wish-that-was-really-a-prayer had been answered.

They talked until dinnertime.

CHAPTER TWELVE

Tuesday at School

Jimmy knew he was off to a bad start at school when, that morning, he found a handwritten note in his desk that said, "Hi, Saint James—Super Christian." It was Tony's handwriting.

At lunch, Jimmy decided to eat by himself. Tony and Brad had other plans and sat down with him.

"So, how's the preaching, Super Christian?" Tony asked. Brad chuckled.

"Leave me alone," Jimmy said.

"Oh, come on, Jimmy. Quit being so serious," Tony said.

"Then quit teasing me," Jimmy said.

"Okay, Saint James, I won't tease you anymore."

Jimmy scowled at Tony.

"We really wanna know more about all this church stuff,"

Tony said, barely keeping the smirk off his face.

Brad leaned close and added, "Are you gonna start wearing one of those white collars like the priests do?"

"He'll wear a blue shirt with a big S in the middle of it," Tony said. "For *Super Christian!*" Then Tony sang the *Superman* theme and stretched out his arms as if he were flying around the table.

Jimmy tried to remember the verse his grandmother had written in the front of his Bible. "Don't let people look down on you. . . . Be an example and behave," or something like that. He stuffed the last of his sandwich into his mouth and got up to leave.

Tony grabbed his arm. "Don't you wanna pray before you go?" he asked with a laugh.

Brad said, "Isn't he supposed to dismiss us with a hymn or something?"

Jimmy jerked his arm away and said through his mouthful of sandwich, "Just leave me alone!"

As he marched away, he heard Brad ask, "What did he say?"

Tony laughed again and said, "I think he said to *weave him a home*."

Jimmy tried to figure out why Tony was being so obnoxious. Okay, so Jimmy had become a Christian. Why did that make Tony so mean? Just a few days ago, they were best friends. Now Tony acted as if they were enemies. What was going on?

Since there was still some lunchtime left, Jimmy walked out to the playground. On the dodgeball court, he saw Jack and

Oscar, with Lucy standing nearby, talking to a group of girls. Jimmy didn't know any of them very well, except that Jack and Lucy went to his church. He wasn't sure about Oscar. Maybe he should try to be friends with them now that he was a Christian.

He was thinking about going over to talk to them when he heard an approaching hissing noise, like air coming out of a balloon. He turned around just as Tony and Brad, arms out-stretched, faced around him like two Superboys. They hissed through their teeth to make it sound as if they were flying through the air.

"It's Super Christian!" Tony announced. "Faster than a speeding Bible!"

"Able to leap tall churches in a single bound!" Brad said.

"It's a bird. . . ."

"It's a plane. . . ."

"Go away!" Jimmy shouted.

"It's Super Christian!" they yelled together as they circled around and around him.

Jimmy tried to move past them, but they stayed with him no matter where he tried to go. "Cut it out!" Jimmy shouted at Tony.

"Super Christian! Super Christian!" Tony said over and over.

Finally, Jimmy had had enough and stuck out a leg to trip one of them. He caught Brad's foot. Brad spun to the ground, landing in a way that knocked the wind out of him.

Tony nearly tripped over the ashen Brad, but he caught himself in time. He angrily pushed Jimmy. "What're you doing, Super Christian?" Tony demanded. "Super Christians aren't supposed to make people trip."

"Leave me alone," Jimmy said through clenched teeth.

"Make me," Tony said and pushed Jimmy again.

"Go away."

"What're you gonna do, cry like you almost did yesterday? Huh, Super Christian?" Tony teased as he pushed Jimmy once more.

Tony's remark wouldn't have been so stinging if Jimmy hadn't felt like crying—but he did. Tony was supposed to be his best friend, and it made no sense that he would act like this.

Jimmy then did the one thing he never thought he'd do. He looked straight into Tony's face, with its twisted smirk and defiant eyes . . .

and punched him in the nose.

Tony's expression of surprise burned itself into Jimmy's memory, but no more so than the way Tony staggered backward, tripped over Brad, who was trying to stand up, and fell flat on his backside.

The image stayed on Jimmy's mind even as Mr. Parks grabbed his arm and led him to the principal's office.

*****

"What did you think you were doing?" George Barclay asked Jimmy as they drove home from the school half an hour later. "Is that your way of bringing people to Jesus—by punching them in the nose?"

"He was teasing me, Dad. He's been teasing me ever since I told him I was a Christian," Jimmy complained.

"So let him tease you. Who cares what he thinks?" George said.

"I do. He's supposed to be my best friend. Why's he being such a creep?"

George shrugged. "Maybe he doesn't like Christians."

Jimmy thought about it, then shook his head. "I never saw him act like this with the other Christian kids at school."

George was thoughtful for a moment. They drove on. Finally he said, "But the other Christian kids at school weren't his best friend, were they?"

"Huh?"

"Think about it, Jimmy. You were best friends, and suddenly you go through a change that Tony's not part of. Since then, he's been teasing you and picking on you, right?"

"Right," Jimmy said.

"And now you're thinking that he's rejected you, right?"

"Well, yeah."

"And what's *he* thinking?" George asked.

"That's what I can't figure out!" Jimmy said.

George rubbed his chin. "I'm just guessing—and I'm not trying to excuse what you two have been doing to each other—but . . . isn't it possible that Tony thinks *you* rejected *him?*"

"What!"

"Sure," George said. "You're a Christian now, and you think Tony should come along with you into your new adventure. But what if Tony's afraid you're going to leave him behind? Maybe he resents what's happened to you because it'll take you away from him."

"But we can still be friends if he'd stop acting like such a jerk!"

"Can you?"

"Yeah!" Jimmy said. Then he thought about it for a moment and added, "I mean, can't we?"

"I don't know," George said with a shrug of his shoulders. "Sometimes Christianity can tear friends—even families—apart."

They pulled into their driveway, and George turned to Jimmy. "You know you'll have to be punished. I can't have you going around punching kids in the nose—even if it seemed like self-defense."

"At this rate, I'm gonna be grounded for life."

"It's going to seem like it. I'm adding *two weeks* to your restriction," George said.

"But Dad!"

"Don't argue. You might get time off for good behavior, but you're going to have to be *really* good."

George opened his door to get out.

Jimmy sat and stewed. Tony had gotten him in trouble *again*.

CHAPTER THIRTEEN

Tuesday Evening at Home

Jimmy went straight to his room and paced around like a lion in a cage. Two more weeks' restriction, and all because of Tony. It wasn't fair!

His mom peeked in on him. "Hi, Jimmy," she said.

"Hi," he said unhappily.

"Sorry you had a bad day."

Jimmy frowned at her.

"Dave left some material on your study desk, if you want to look at it," she continued. "Considering what happened today, you should probably read it." And she retreated from the room.

Jimmy went to his desk. He wished he'd been there when Dave came. He needed to talk to Dave or Jacob. He frowned again and thought how stupid it was that Jacob was taught at home. If he'd been at school with Jimmy, he could have helped Jimmy deal with Tony and Brad.

"To Jimmy B," said the writing on the large, yellow envelope. He flipped up the clasp on the back and dumped out the contents. A small paperback book fell on top of his normal junk. "Tips for New Christians," the cover said.

In his frame of mind, Jimmy didn't have the patience to read the book. He simply flipped through the various sections about the importance of Bible study, prayer, sharing the faith—and one particular section about the life of a new Christian.

"Purity is a vital part of the new Christian's life," the book said. "You need to be pure in what you see and hear and do. As a new believer, you don't want to expose yourself to anything that will stunt your growth in Jesus. With a prayerful heart, look closely at the books you read, the television shows you watch, the music you listen to. Maybe it's time to clean your house—and your soul—of risky, un-Christian material."

Jimmy had the sense to know that as long as he was mad at Tony, he wouldn't have a very "prayerful heart." But he glanced over at his cassette player and saw the tapes Tony had played the night Jimmy smoked the cigar.

He picked one up and thought about purity. *This'll stunt my growth in Jesus*, he said to himself. Clenching the thin tape between his fingers, he angrily pulled it out of the case. It fell to the floor in ribbons.

It made Jimmy feel good. *Pure*, he thought.

He pulled the tape out of another cassette. And another.

And another—until he exhausted his own collection and wondered how pure his parents' and sister's collections were.

*****

"I'll kill him!" Donna Barclay said.

"All right, let's not get carried away," George said.

Jimmy sat on the living room sofa and watched his judges and jury. He was no longer mad at Tony. That emotion had been moved to a position of lesser importance now that his family was ready to hand him over to a juvenile detention agency.

"When did you do it?" Mary asked in a bewildered tone. "How did you do it so *fast?*"

"We were in the family room watching the movie," Donna offered. "That's when he did it. We thought he was upstairs doing his homework or . . . or reading his Bible."

George leaned against the doorway into the dining room. "I can't keep up with you anymore, Jimmy," he said. "Today you punched your best friend in the nose, and tonight . . . What possessed you?"

"We don't want anything in the house that'll stunt our growth in Jesus, right?"

George and Mary looked at each other as if to decide who would answer. George shrugged helplessly.

"Right," Mary said. "But you should leave the decision of what will stunt *our* growth to *us.*"

"Did you see what he did to my room?" Donna growled.

"He took down my posters! He went through my books! He tore apart my cassette tapes!"

"Not the *Christian* ones," Jimmy said in his own defense.

"That's not the point! You're supposed to keep your mitts off my stuff!" Donna insisted.

"Okay, calm down," George said to Donna. Then he turned his attention to Jimmy. "Son, I appreciate your enthusiasm—"

"Enthusiasm!" Donna cried out as if she might tear at her hair in exasperation.

"Yes," George said. "If I remember right, enthusiasm is normal for a new Christian. Don't you remember, Donna? When you became a Christian, you tried to plaster Christian bumper stickers all over the car. And I don't think you asked us first, either."

Donna slumped back in her chair. "That was different."

"No, it wasn't. You were enthusiastic about your newfound belief—just like Jimmy. But what we need is *balance* and *consideration*. So, Jimmy, next time you get the . . . uh, inspiration to purge the house of things you consider less than Christian, talk to us first, okay?"

"Yes, sir."

"Where did you put Donna's things?" Mary asked.

"In the garage. I put everybody's stuff in a box next to the garbage can," Jimmy answered.

George shook his head as if he hadn't heard correctly. "*Everybody's* stuff? Which everybody's stuff?"

"Yours and Mom's," Jimmy said.

Mary was on the edge of her seat. *"Our stuff?"* she asked. "You went through our stuff, too?"

"Yeah! You guys really oughtta be ashamed of yourselves," Jimmy said.

But his words were lost in the commotion as George, Mary, and Donna raced to the garage.

CHAPTER FOURTEEN

Wednesday Afternoon

Jimmy didn't see Tony again until the next day at recess. He had just finished a round of dodgeball when he noticed that Tony was sitting on the sidelines, watching him. Mr. Parks blew the whistle for everyone to go back into the building.

"Hey, Jimmy," Tony said as he ran up to him.

Jimmy prepared himself for another clash, maybe even a fight. "What?" he asked.

Tony walked at Jimmy's side. "Slow down, I wanna talk to you."

"What about?"

"You know," Tony said.

At a glance, Jimmy noticed that the punch in the nose hadn't done any damage. He felt a twinge of disappointment that he didn't have more power in his punch. "No, I don't."

"What happened yesterday. Do I have to spell it out?" Tony asked.

At that moment, Jimmy realized that in all the years of their friendship, they had never had to say they were sorry to each other. Even when they got on each other's nerves or had an argument, apologies were simply understood, not spoken.

"Look," Tony said, "I shouldn't have teased you so much. It's just that . . . well . . . I don't get this Christian thing. That's all."

Dad was right, Jimmy thought. Tony acted like a jerk because he felt Jimmy was rejecting him—leaving him behind by heading into a new experience. So that was it. That was Tony's apology. "Forget about it," Jimmy said.

They walked silently to the door. "A bunch of us are going to the gazebo in McAlister Park after school," Tony finally said. "Tim Ryan has something he wants to show us. He says it's real cool. You wanna come?"

Tim Ryan was well known for finding all kinds of neat things for Jimmy and his friends to look at. A few weeks ago, he had brought bullets from his dad's gun. But Jimmy said, "My parents said I have to go straight home after school. I'm still on restriction, remember?"

"Just tell 'em you stayed after school to do homework or something. You can figure it out," Tony suggested.

Jimmy knew this was like offering him a peace pipe. It was a way to be friends the way they were before. If he said no, it'd be the same as hitting Tony in the nose all over again. He had to say yes. "Well . . . okay. I'll try."

"Good," Tony said, and he spun on his heel to go to class.

*****

The gazebo in McAlister Park was a popular place in the summer, even though it was out of the way. It was shaped like a large, round, wooden porch with open sides and a white roof. Bands often played there, politicians made speeches from it, and couples sat in it with their arms around each other while dreaming the warm days away. As the cloudy afternoons of September rolled into October, that part of the park saw fewer people come through. It was a perfect meeting place for a group of kids.

By the time Jimmy got there, Tony, Brad, and a few of their other friends were gathered in the center of the gazebo. "Tim's not here yet," Tony explained when Jimmy joined them.

"What's he got?" Jimmy asked as he dropped his school books onto one of the benches that lined the gazebo.

"You'll see," Tony said.

"There he is!" Gary Holman said, pointing.

They turned to look. Tim ran toward them, all smiles as he carried a brown bag. He took the stairs up to the gazebo two at a time and was breathless when he reached the other boys. "Hi, guys," he gasped.

"Did you get them?" Tony asked.

"Yeah!" Tim said. "My dad almost caught me, though."

"What is it?" Jimmy asked.

"Here." Tim opened the bag for everyone to look. Inside

were strings of firecrackers, a small rocket, matches, and a small can of lighter fluid.

"Great!" Tony said.

"What's the lighter fluid for?" Cory Sleazak asked.

"Oh, just in case it's too windy to light the fuses," Tim answered. "I figured it'll help keep everything burning."

Tony took charge. "Gary, keep an eye out. We don't wanna set these things off when somebody's coming."

"We're setting them *all* off?" Jimmy asked.

Tony smiled and said, "Yeah! Fourth of July at the beginning of October!"

"The noise'll make people come running. We'll get in trouble," Jimmy said.

Tony frowned at him. "Not if we light the fuse and run, you idiot. We'll soak the long fuse in lighter fluid so it'll burn while we run. Then we can watch the fireworks from the woods." He turned to Tim and instructed, "Let's get it going."

"I don't think it's a good idea," Jimmy said, knowing full well that he would look like a party pooper.

"Quit being a spoilsport!" Cory said. "Or should we call you *Saint James?*"

"Shut up," Tony snapped at Cory. "He's not like that. Now come on, let's put everything on the floor and get it ready."

Jimmy watched silently as Tony and Tim stretched the string of firecrackers along the wooden floor, paying careful attention to the fuse.

"What should we do with the rocket?" Tim asked.

"Put it at the end of the firecrackers so its fuse'll catch when they go off," Tony said.

"Let's point it toward the field," Cory suggested.

Tony grabbed the rocket. "Good idea!" he said. He positioned it so it would shoot through the opening between the bannister and the roof. He tied the rocket fuse to the firecracker fuse so it would catch.

"Get back, I'm gonna pour the lighter fluid on it now," Tim said.

Everyone took a few steps back. Tim poured the fluid onto the firecracker fuse.

He giggled as he said, "I'm spilling it."

"Put some on the rocket fuse," Tony told him. "Hurry or it'll evaporate."

Tim laughed as he spilled more of the fluid. Finally he just turned the can upside down and poured it all over the firecrackers and rocket. "That'll help it go up faster," he said.

Jimmy didn't know a lot about lighter fluid, but something told him this was a bad idea. Even if it evaporated quickly in the cool breeze, it might make the fireworks explode faster than they wanted and hit them before they could run. Jimmy was about to protest when Tony lit a match.

"Run!" he shouted and threw the match at the fuse. It caught immediately. The kids ran out of the gazebo and toward the woods about 25 yards away. Jimmy ducked behind a large tree with Tony and watched.

From where they stood, Jimmy could see the smoke—

more than there should've been for just a fuse. "What if the gazebo catches on fire?" Jimmy whispered to Tony.

Tony looked as if the idea hadn't occurred to him. He shrugged.

Suddenly *Pop!*—then another *Pop!*—then *Pop! Pop! Pop! Pop!* as the string of firecrackers sparked and exploded like a gangster's machine gun. From behind various trees, the kids pointed and laughed.

"That's *better* than the Fourth of July!" Tony shouted.

The firecrackers were still banging away when the rocket hissed loudly and took off. But the trajectory was all wrong. Instead of shooting toward the field, it spun and spiraled upward into the roof of the gazebo. Jimmy watched in wonder.

Kaboom! The blast echoed throughout the park. Smoke poured out the top of the gazebo.

"It's on fire!" Jimmy gasped. "It's on fire!"

"Get out of here!" Tony yelled and raced into the woods. The rest of the kids followed. Jimmy stood mesmerized where he was, not sure of what to do as smoke blew from the gazebo. "Jimmy! Run!" Tony screamed from a distance.

It was enough. Jimmy panicked and ran home.

*****

"Oh, God, I'm sorry I'm sorry I'm sorry I'm sorry," Jimmy puffed as he ran. He didn't know which direction Tony and the other kids went, nor did he care. He shouldn't have gone to the gazebo, he knew. He shouldn't have let them light firecrackers. *The gazebo's going to burn down, and it's all my fault.*

What should he do? Tell his parents? Call the fire department? He didn't know. What was the *Christian* thing to do? "God, help me. I'm sorry I'm sorry I'm sorry. . . ."

By the time he reached his front door, he knew he had to tell his parents. *They* could call the fire department. But Jimmy figured the gazebo would be burned down by that time. And then he'd be an arsonist and go to jail.

He burst through the front door on the verge of tears. In the living room, several heads turned in his direction. He stopped dead in his tracks. His mom and dad, Donna, Dave, and Jacob were sitting with very serious expressions on their faces.

They already know! Jimmy thought.

"Jimmy!" his dad said. "Where've you been? We've been looking for you."

As an automatic response, Jimmy nearly said he'd stayed late at school to do his homework. Then he realized he didn't have his books with him—he had left them at the gazebo, where they were either ashes or evidence for the fire chief. That was the end. His life was over. He began to sob.

Mary rushed to Jimmy and wrapped her arms around him. "Aw, that's all right, Jimmy. It'll be okay." His ear pressed against her, he heard her say to the others, "I guess he got the message at school."

Jimmy looked up at her through misty eyes. "Message?" He was confused.

"About your grandmother," she said and stroked his hair. "She's taken a turn for the worse. We have to leave right away."

CHAPTER FIFTEEN

Wednesday Evening

Things were happening too fast for Jimmy's mind to cope. Suddenly he had to jump from the gazebo to his grandmother.

"I need you to pack," his mom told him. Then she glanced around and asked, "Where are your schoolbooks?"

"I left them—"

"You're going to need them," she interrupted. "Your teacher told me what homework you can do while we're gone."

"I'll drive you back to school," his dad said.

Jimmy opened his mouth to tell them his books weren't *at* school. They were at the burned-down gazebo. But Dave spoke first.

"I know you have a lot of things to do," Dave said. He and Jacob stood up. "How about if we take him to get his books?

That'll be one less thing for you to worry about. Besides, I'd like to talk to him before you go."

"If you don't mind," George said.

"I don't," Dave said with a smile. "Let's go, Jimmy."

Jimmy felt as if he were caught in a strong current that carried him down a river. But whether he was headed for a peaceful lake or a rocky waterfall, he couldn't be sure.

Dave hugged Mary, then George, then Donna. "God be with you," he said. "We'll pray for you."

"Thanks," everyone muttered.

With a hand on each of their shoulders, Dave guided Jimmy and Jacob to the door. "I'll have him back in a few minutes," he said.

*****

In the car, Jimmy confessed to Dave that his books weren't at school but at the gazebo.

"Gazebo! In McAlister Park?" Dave asked.

Jimmy nodded.

"What were you doing at the gazebo? I thought you were on restriction. Weren't you supposed to come straight home after school?"

"Yeah," Jimmy answered. "But I didn't."

From his place behind the steering wheel, Dave glanced across the seat at Jimmy. "Then you didn't get the message about your grandmother."

"No," Jimmy said.

"So you weren't crying about her. You were crying about something else."

Jimmy's chest tightened. "Yeah."

"Why were you so upset?"

"You'll see," Jimmy said.

*****

They parked the car at the edge of the park and got out. Jimmy looked around for some sign of the fire department or police, but everything seemed quiet as usual. They walked down the path through the woods to the gazebo.

It was still there.

Dave and Jacob both noticed Jimmy's wide-eyed expression as they approached it. "Jimmy?" Dave inquired.

"It's still here," he whispered.

They mounted the steps. "Of course it's still here. What did you think?" Dave asked.

"There're your books," Jacob said. They were still sitting on one of the benches that lined the gazebo's bannister. Jimmy picked them up. There was no sign that they had been touched by fire.

"That's a shame," Dave said. He pointed to the floor of the gazebo.

Jimmy looked down. There were bits of paper, black powder, and scorch marks where the firecrackers had been. The marks led to a larger black mark—a black circle that looked as if someone had dropped a bottle of ink on the floor and it had exploded. *The rocket*, Jimmy knew. He glanced up at the roof. It was also scarred with black marks like those on the floor. Other than that, the gazebo looked the same as it always did. Obviously their prank caused a lot of smoke but no fire. Jimmy slumped onto the bench with relief.

"What do you know about this?" Dave asked.

Jimmy gazed up at Dave and confessed everything.

*****

"You have to tell your parents," Dave said as they drove home.

"I know," Jimmy said.

"Don't make excuses. Just tell them what happened."

"Okay."

"I'm sure they'll understand," Dave said.

Jimmy wasn't so sure of that.

"They'll probably make you pay for the damage," Dave said. "Maybe your friends'll help."

Fat chance, Jimmy thought.

Dave stopped at a traffic light and studied Jimmy. "This isn't unusual, you know. You're going to have battles with your old friends. They're going to want you to act like you always did, and you won't be able to. It'll cause a lot of conflict—more than you've had already. Jacob knows."

Jimmy turned in the seat to look at Jacob, who sat in the back.

"My best friend wasn't a Christian," Jacob said. "And he

didn't care when I became a Christian. But he thought I'd keep doing all the stuff we used to do, and I couldn't. I mean, we weren't *bad* kids, but everything changed. I wanted to do more things at church, and he wouldn't come with me."

"What happened?" Jimmy asked.

"He stopped being my friend," Jacob said sadly.

"But Tony and I have been best friends since the first grade!" Jimmy said. "I don't have to stop being his friend just because I'm a Christian, do I?"

"If he expects you to do the kind of mischief you did today, how *can* you stay friends with him?" Dave asked.

Jimmy settled back in his seat and thought about it. He didn't have an answer. *There has to be a way for us to stay friends*, he thought.

"You need courage," Dave said. "We'll pray that God will give you the courage to do the right thing. Go on, Jacob."

Jacob prayed for Jimmy, for him to have courage, for Tony, and for Jimmy's family as they went to visit his sick grandmother. It was a simple, heartfelt prayer that sounded strange to Jimmy's ears, particularly since it came from someone Jimmy's age.

How come it seems so easy for Jacob to talk to God? Jimmy wondered. "I wish I could pray like that," he said after Jacob finished.

"You will eventually," Dave said. They pulled into Jimmy's driveway.

"When?" Jimmy asked.

Dave chuckled. "Be patient," he said. "You've only been a Christian for a few days. Give yourself a chance to grow."

"Does that mean I'll be like Jacob—or you?"

"Wait a minute," Dave said. "I don't think you'd want to be like either one of us."

"But I do! You guys are so smart. You always know the right thing to do."

Dave tapped the steering wheel with his fingers. "No, Jimmy. That's not true. We make a lot of mistakes. You only get to see us when we're on our best behavior. Right, Jacob?"

Jacob nodded.

"I don't believe you," Jimmy said.

"Don't do this to us, Jimmy," Dave said with a sudden seriousness. "Keep your eyes on Jesus. If you look at us, you'll only be disappointed. We have problems; we make mistakes. Keep your eyes on the One who saved you, okay?"

Jimmy said okay, but his heart wasn't in it.

Dave playfully pushed at Jimmy. "Now go on. And don't forget to tell your parents about the gazebo."

"I promise," Jimmy said and climbed out of the car.

He watched Dave and Jacob drive away. He had no idea it would be the last time he'd see them.

CHAPTER SIXTEEN

Wednesday Night and Thursday

With a four-hour drive ahead of them, Jimmy decided it would be better to tell his parents about the gazebo after they were well on their way.

When he broke the news, his mom was instantly upset and couldn't believe he'd do such a thing. His dad said he appreciated Jimmy's honesty, but that Jimmy would have to pay for any damage *and* plan for an extra punishment when they got home.

Donna rolled her eyes and said, "It seems you're getting in more trouble now than you did before you became a Christian."

Jimmy hadn't really thought about it, but now that Donna brought up the idea, he had to agree. It seemed *everything* started going wrong after he went to Dave's club meeting. He said yes to Jesus and had since made Tony, his other friends, and his family mad at him, and now his grandma was sicker, too. It was as if he couldn't win no matter what he did. What was the point of being a Christian if things weren't going to get better?

These thoughts swirled in his head as the lights from passing streetlamps and buildings mixed the shadows in the darkness of the backseat. They lulled him to sleep.

"Jimmy," his dad said, bringing Jimmy back to consciousness.

"Yeah?" Jimmy looked up to see his dad's eyes in the rearview mirror.

"You have no idea how thankful to God I am for your newfound faith. Hang in there."

*****

They arrived at Grandma Barclay's house in a town called Newberry just before midnight. It wasn't the house George or his brother and sister grew up in. Grandma had sold that house after Grandpa Barclay died. This was a smaller, cottage-sized house in the middle of a village for retired people. George identified himself to the security guard at the gate and was allowed to pass. He used his key to get in the house itself. There was a note from Mildred, one of Jimmy's grandmother's friends, saying that she'd made them sandwiches and would call in the morning. Grandma Barclay was in the intensive care section of the hospital, the note finished.

The Barclays sleepily ate the sandwiches and organized

who was sleeping where. Mom and Dad slept in the guest room. Donna got the couch in the small living room. Jimmy used his sleeping bag on the floor. No one wanted to sleep in Grandma's bed.

The next morning, Mildred arrived as they were having breakfast in the tiny kitchen. She was a lively old woman with wild, silver hair and dancing, blue eyes. She told them Grandma Barclay had collapsed the morning before, with a sharp pain in her abdomen. Her doctor at the hospital said there was no doubt about it now—the cancer had returned. This time there would be no therapy. There was nothing anyone could do but pray.

Jimmy remembered that he had prayed for his grandmother a few days before. *A lot of good it did*, he thought.

They drove to the Rock Creek Hospital. Jimmy didn't like hospitals much. They had a peculiar smell, the nurses weren't very friendly in their starched white uniforms, and patients sometimes moaned from their rooms. Hospitals gave Jimmy the creeps.

Intensive care was a quiet area with a lot of softly beeping equipment and gadgets Jimmy couldn't identify. The nurses and doctors looked tired. After George assured the nurse that they were all family who'd traveled a long way to see his mother, she said she'd bend the rules a little and let them all in to see Victoria. Jimmy wondered who Victoria was, then remembered that was his grandmother's name. He'd forgotten that grandparents once had first names like that.

As they walked toward Grandma Barclay, Jimmy caught sight of other patients in the ward. They were young and old. Most of them lay very still. One man with white skin looked as if he had died. Jimmy hoped the nurses knew.

They came to Jimmy's grandmother. He hardly recognized her. Her normally clean and styled hair was matted and greasy. Her skin was a pasty color, and without her makeup, she looked a hundred years older than she was. She had tubes and wire hanging from her face and dangling from odd angles under her sheets.

Mary's eyes filled with tears. Donna put her hand over her mouth. George touched his mother's arm tenderly. Jimmy watched with a mixture of wonder and fear. He was far, far away from any of the things that gave him comfort: his room, his school, his Odyssey, his youth, his future. There his world didn't include the old and the dying.

"If you were to die tonight . . ." the booklet said.

Grandma Barclay slowly opened her eyes. A shadow of a smile moved across her lips when she saw George. "You came," she whispered in a distant voice.

"Hi, Mom," George said. "We're all here."

Grandma tried to adjust her head so she could see them. "Mary . . . Donna . . ." She lifted her hand weakly. "Where's Jimmy?"

Jimmy moved toward the bed so she could see him.

"Ah," she coughed. "I knew it would happen. I always knew it." She wiggled her fingers for Jimmy to come closer. He did. She touched his hand. "I've been praying for you since before you were born. I knew you would meet the Lord. I prayed every day."

Jimmy felt tears burning at the backs of his eyes. "Thanks, Grandma."

"I want to talk to you," she said. "There are . . . things . . . I want to say to you."

"When you're stronger, Mom," George said.

She smiled and closed her eyes. "No strength until . . . later."

George quietly ushered the family out of the room.

George insisted on staying at the hospital—at his mother's side—if they would let him. But he gave Mary, Donna, and Jimmy the okay to leave for a while. Mary and Donna conspired to go to the mall. Faced with the prospect of shopping for clothes with his mother and sister or watching TV in the waiting room, Jimmy opted for the TV. Besides, he was curious about what his grandmother wanted to say to him and didn't want to miss the chance to talk if she woke up.

An hour or so later—after Jimmy had sampled one of the dried chocolate cupcakes in the vending machine and watched all he could stand of the TV soap operas—his dad came back. "She's awake," he said. "She wants to talk to you."

Jimmy leapt to his feet.

"Now, son, don't do anything to excite her, all right? Take it easy."

"Okay," Jimmy said. He followed his dad back through the corridors to his grandmother's room. When they reached the door, George gestured for Jimmy to go in and walked away toward the nurses' station.

She looked better this time. Someone had brushed her hair, and she was propped up in a way that made it appear as if she were at home in bed with a book. Jimmy smiled at her as he rounded the bed. She smiled wearily back at him. "Hi, Jimmy," she said in the same distant voice he'd heard before. It was her voice, but it seemed to come from another place.

"Hi, Grandma," Jimmy said. "How're you feeling?"

"Awful, but I'll get over it," she said, chuckling. "How are you doing?"

"Okay," he said.

She patted the mattress as a signal for him to come closer. "I mean, how are you doing now that you've met Jesus?"

Jimmy was puzzled. "I asked Him into my heart, Grandma," he said. "But it doesn't feel like I really met Him."

"Those feelings will come," she said. "Keep your faith and the feelings usually follow."

"Is that what you wanted to tell me?" Jimmy asked.

Grandma closed her eyes as if she felt a deep pain somewhere. Then she opened them again. "I have so much to tell you. I wish we had years. I would love to . . . to see you grow up in your faith."

"You will, Grandma. We're praying for you!" Jimmy said.

"Good," she said, her voice raspy and broken. "Pray hard. Not because I'll get better, but because you should pray. Learn to talk to God, Jimmy. Talk to Him all the time. He's listening.

He's always listening. Things won't always work out the way you want, but He's always there. He knows what's best."

Jimmy leaned forward, his elbows pressing into the mattress. "You have to get better, Grandma. It wouldn't be fair for you to leave me right after I became a Christian." He paused as the full reality of the situation came to him. She was going to die and leave him. "I need you."

Grandma turned her head so she could look Jimmy in the eyes. For a moment, they seemed as bright and clear as when she was healthy—the way Jimmy always remembered her. "You don't need me," she said firmly. "You need Jesus."

"But Jesus isn't here," he said. "And I don't have anybody else."

"You have your family. You have your church. You have friends—some you haven't even met yet. Jesus is in them." She raised a finger and pointed at Jimmy's chest. "You have Him in there."

"But it isn't fair. I didn't know it was gonna be this hard."

She coughed and grabbed Jimmy's hand. "Fair has nothing to do with it. Look at me, Jimmy. Nobody said the Christian life was fair—or easy. Nothing in this world is fair or easy. Growing old and dying of cancer isn't fair or easy. But God is good."

She gasped and lay back with her eyes closed. She still had hold of Jimmy's hand. He waited, worried she might die right then and there.

A minute passed, and she opened her eyes again. She whispered, "You want to meet Jesus? Well, sometimes the Lord has to strip everything away from us before we can truly meet Him. And sometimes it really hurts. I felt it when your grandfather died, then my brothers and sisters, then my friends . . . and then my own body stopped working a little at a time. It's the Lord's way of getting me to pay attention. He's taking it all away from me so He can give it back in a newer, more wonderful way. It's like He gives us a good, hard scrubbing—and it hurts a little—so we'll be cleaned up to see Him face to face." She squeezed Jimmy's hand. "You see, He strips it away *here* so He can give it back to me nice and new *there*."

A chill ran up and down Jimmy's spine. Those were the same words Dave had used the night Jimmy said yes to Jesus. It led to a new life for Jimmy. In a strange way, Jimmy now understood how it would lead to a new life for his grandmother—a new life in that other place where God lives. But it still meant she would leave him, and he didn't want that. Not now, not yet.

"Oh, Jimmy," his grandmother said, and he saw a small tear slip from her eye and slide down her temple. "I'm so happy for you . . . all the adventures you have ahead of you. I'll be watching. . . ."

She closed her eyes again. Her grip on Jimmy's hand relaxed completely—and let go.

*****

That evening, Jimmy, Donna, and Mary had dinner at a restaurant with Uncle Donald and Aunt Gwen, George's younger brother and sister. They had arrived that afternoon. Jimmy's dad insisted they should go while he stayed at the hospital, as long as they promised to bring him back something to eat. Since Uncle Donald, Aunt Gwen, and their families rarely came to Odyssey, they had the usual conversation about how big the kids had gotten and how they were doing in school and what the adults liked or didn't like about their jobs. Jimmy zoned out. He thought about his grandmother and once again prayed that God would let her live.

Toward the end of the meal, Mary realized she hadn't asked George what he wanted her to bring back for him. She excused herself and went to the pay phone. Jimmy and Uncle Donald exchanged knowing looks as Aunt Gwen and Donna started talking about hairstyles. The minutes ticked away. Jimmy glanced over at the pay phone just in time to see his mother hang up the receiver and wipe tears from her eyes.

Jimmy knew.

Mary reached the table and put on the brave face that Jimmy had seen at other times when there was bad news. "I'm so sorry," she said, choking back the tears. "Grandma died 10 minutes ago."

CHAPTER SEVENTEEN

Friday and Saturday

Over the next two days, Jimmy battled more against boredom than against grief. George, Donald, and Gwen made arrangements at the funeral home. Distant family members came to the house, cried, and left again. Errands were run. Members of Grandma's church brought food. Friends dropped in to pay their respects.

Amidst all the activity, Jimmy didn't have anything to do. He tried to watch television on Grandma's portable black-and-white, but she didn't have cable, and the aerial only picked up three snowy channels. He made an effort to finish his homework, but the buzz of activity distracted him. And there was nowhere to go in the middle of a retirement village.

Friday evening arrived, and Mary handed Jimmy his Easter suit from last year. He didn't even know she had packed it—

and only then realized that she had because she had known Grandma would die.

"Where are we going?" he asked.

"The viewing," she replied.

"Viewing?"

Mary explained that it was a time for everyone to see Grandma in the coffin at the funeral home—a time to offer comfort to the family and to say good-bye to Grandma. "Don't you remember when your grandfather died?" she asked.

Jimmy didn't. He was just five years old when that happened and had only the vaguest memory of black suits and a long, black hearse at a graveyard.

The funeral home smelled like flowers. So did the funeral director. He took Jimmy's hand in a cold grip and shook it while he said in a soft, deep voice how sorry he was about "Victoria's passing."

Dad guided Jimmy, Donna, and Mary into a cozy room with dim lighting and chairs, lamps, and tables that looked as if they belonged in somebody's house. Near the wall on the far end of the room sat a long, brown coffin. Grandma's head was barely visible above the shiny box and the lacy linen it rested on. Donna froze in her steps. "I can't go," she cried.

Mary hugged her and took her aside. "Whenever you're ready, Donna," she said. "It's okay."

George looked at Jimmy. "Do you want to wait?" he asked.

"No," Jimmy said. "Let's go."

George and Jimmy approached the coffin. At first, Jimmy

thought someone had made a mistake. It wasn't his grand-mother. But he looked closer and realized it was. She looked as though somebody had done a bad job of making a wax mannequin of her. Her hair was all wrong. Her eyes looked painted closed. Her lips were stretched too tight.

"It doesn't look like her," Jimmy whispered to his dad.

George put his hand on Jimmy's shoulder. "In a way, it's not really her," he said. "This is just an empty shell where she used to be."

Jimmy carefully studied the face in the coffin. *An empty shell where she used to be.* Her hands were folded across her waist. Jimmy reached up and touched them. Waxy and cold. All life had gone to another place—that place where God lives. And for a moment, Jimmy imagined her rushing into the arms of his grandfather, shaking hands with all those friends who'd left her, and turning to see the One she longed to see face to face.

Jimmy patted her hand and asked Jesus to say hello to her for him.

*****

The funeral service on Saturday was a strange mixture of joy and tears. It was as if they couldn't make up their minds how they felt, Jimmy thought later. One minute a pastor was talking about the joy of going home. The next minute, family and friends wept as they said how much they'd miss Grandma and her wonderful sense of humor, her faith, her love, or her homemade cookies.

George got up and captured what Jimmy felt most when he said, "Our loss is heaven's gain. For those of us who know Jesus, we can be assured that this isn't good-bye, but simply 'Until we meet again.'"

Jimmy cried when he heard that and felt a flood of grief rise up within and pour out of his eyes. Grandma was gone. Gone for good. He couldn't stop crying until they drove to the gravesite and threw flowers onto the coffin as it was lowered into the ground.

After that, Jimmy brooded that it still wasn't fair. Now that he was a Christian, it would've made a lot more sense for God to let his grandmother live so she could help him. He still didn't know what to do about Tony. He didn't know about a lot of things. His mood sank into self-pity. He'd only been a Christian for a week, and he had probably lost his best friend and definitely his grandmother. What else could go wrong?

He fought with Donna in the car on the way home. She was listening to music on her portable stereo with headphones. Jimmy thought the tinny guitars and drums that leaked from her ears would drive him nuts. He jerked at the headphones and told Donna to turn down the volume. She told him to lay off and pushed him away. He pushed her back. They yelled at each other.

Dad pulled the car over to the side of the road. "Stop it!" he shouted at them. "This is tough enough without you two acting like babies!"

The harshness of his voice brought wide-eyed silence from

Jimmy, Donna, and even Mary.

Dad turned away from them, lowered his head onto the steering wheel, and let the tears flow. Mary moved close to him, put her arm around his back, leaned her head against his shoulder, and cried with him. It struck Jimmy that he hadn't seen his dad cry at the hospital, the funeral home, or even Grandma's house.

"I'm sorry," George said. And he kept crying.

Donna glared at Jimmy and whispered, "See what you've done!"

Jimmy felt awful for being so selfish. *What else could go wrong?* he asked himself again. *Nothing*, he answered. *This is as bad as it gets.*

CHAPTER EIGHTEEN

Sunday

Jimmy's mom tightened the belt on her dress. "I don't know if I can handle everybody saying how sorry they are," she said. "I'll cry, I just know it."

The family was back in Odyssey. They were getting ready for church.

"Just take some extra tissues," George advised and kissed his wife on the cheek.

"My purse is stuffed to the top," she replied.

Jimmy drained the last of the milk from his cereal bowl. He was eager to get to church so he could talk to Dave or Jacob. He felt confused about a lot of things—his grandma's death, how to decide about his friendship with Tony, why so many things went wrong after he became a Christian—and he knew they'd tell him what to do.

"Donna, let's go!" George called out.

The Barclay family got into the car and drove to church for what should have been a normal service. It wasn't.

*****

Jimmy looked for some sign of Dave or Jacob in the Sunday school assembly. He couldn't find either of them. He sat down in the auditorium and waited for Dave to take the podium as he usually did. Instead, Mr. Lucas led the morning devotional and prayer.

Jimmy went to class distracted and annoyed. He bumped into Lucy and asked if she had seen Dave or Jacob. She hadn't but said that rumors were flying all over the place about where they were.

"Where are they?" Jimmy asked.

"Kidnapped by aliens if you want to believe Jack Davis," she said and walked off.

Jimmy's mood worsened. Maybe they took the day off. But that didn't make sense. Dave was an assistant pastor—he couldn't be allowed to take Sundays off!

In between Sunday school and church, Jimmy saw his dad. "I can't find Dave or Jacob!" Jimmy said.

"Really?" George said. "Maybe they're gone for the weekend."

"But they *can't* be gone! I wanna talk to them!"

George laughed. "I'm sure they would've canceled their plans if they'd known."

"Find out, will you, Dad? Please?"

"Okay, there's Tom Riley. He should know—he's a deacon. I'll see you in church in a minute." George strode off.

How could they leave me like this? Jimmy fumed. *They knew my grandmother was sick. How could they take a vacation when my grandmother died?*

Jimmy walked into the sanctuary and dropped himself onto the pew next to his mom.

"Well, hello, Mr. Happy," she said.

Jimmy grunted.

George arrived just as the organist started the first hymn. Jimmy looked at him expectantly. George's brow was furrowed into several worried lines.

"Dad?" Jimmy whispered.

"I'll tell you after church," George said.

"*Now*, Dad. *Please*. Are they on vacation?"

"No," George said. "They're gone."

"What!" Jimmy said so loudly that people around them turned to look.

George gently took Jimmy's arm and led him into the hall. "Look, son," he said when they were away from the sanctuary, "I need you to be calm, okay? Pray that God will help you be calm."

Jimmy was worried. "Be calm? But what did you mean—"

"They're gone, Jimmy. Dave and Jacob left the church."

Jimmy's mouth fell open.

George continued, "Do you remember Jan? Dave's wife?"

"Yeah."

"She wasn't happy. Do you understand? She didn't like being a minister's wife. So she left them right after we went to see Grandma. Rather than put the church through a difficult time, Dave and Jacob went back to Dave's family in California." George kept his grip on Jimmy's arm, as if he thought Jimmy might pass out.

"All the way to California?" Jimmy asked weakly.

"Yes."

"But . . . they didn't say good-bye. I didn't get to say anything to them."

"I know." George knelt down next to his son. "They wanted it to happen fast and quietly to stop any gossip. Now do you see why I wanted you to pray?"

Jimmy understood. And he *did* pray. He asked God, "Why are You doing this to me?"

CHAPTER NINETEEN

Sunday Afternoon

I know how tough this week has been for you," Jimmy's dad said to him after their Sunday dinner, as Jimmy lay on his bed. "You've been through a lot."

Jimmy didn't say anything. He had hardly said a word since he found out about Dave and Jacob. All he wanted to do was mope.

George rested his hand on Jimmy's arm. "We've had our share of losses. But . . . that's part of life. We gain family and friends, and we lose them."

Not all in one week, Jimmy thought.

"Your mom and I talked about it, and we're going to give you a break this afternoon," Dad said. "Consider it a short reprieve from your restriction—an escape. Go take a walk or something. Try to . . . I don't know . . . use the time to pray.

Maybe that'll help." He stood up and headed for the door.

"Thanks, Dad," Jimmy said and rolled off his bed. *A walk might be good*, he thought. *A chance to get out of the house.* He tugged on his shoes and grabbed his jacket. But where would he walk? Would he go to Tony's house?

No. He wasn't ready for Tony.

So he was allowed to leave the house, but he didn't have anywhere to go. He felt even more depressed as he walked out the front door and into the cloudy October afternoon.

He thought about the past week as he walked: all the trouble he'd been in with his family and his best friend. Then he lost his grandmother and two people he had *hoped* would be his friends.

He felt completely alone.

Is this what saying yes to Jesus means—walking alone on a Sunday afternoon, with no one to talk to and nowhere to go? he wondered.

He thought about Tony again. He hadn't lost Tony. Not yet. But could he stay friends with Tony and still be a Christian? Or maybe the real question was this: Did he really want to be a Christian if he *couldn't* stay friends with Tony?

It'd be easy enough to forget it, right? Just tell everybody it was a dumb idea—being a Christian caused too many problems—and give it up. Yeah, his family would be disappointed, but they'd get over it. Things could go back to the way they were.

Jimmy looked around and realized he was walking in

McAlister Park. He felt a twinge of guilt as he remembered the incident at the gazebo. He hadn't talked to Tony since it happened. He wondered what Tony was thinking. Did word get around the school about Jimmy's grandmother? Did Tony know?

Again, Jimmy felt alone. And restless. He wanted to do something. He wanted to be normal again and run around with his friends and quit having so many things go wrong. Could he quit being a Christian now? Would God let him change his mind?

"Hey, Jimmy."

Jimmy nearly jumped out of his skin. Tony stood directly in front of him. "What're you doing here?" Jimmy asked.

"I was gonna ask you the same question," Tony said. "I stopped by your house, and your dad said you took a walk. I thought you were on restriction."

"They let me off today."

"Why didn't you come over?"

"I was going to, but . . ." Jimmy sighed and started to walk again. "I'm confused."

Tony stayed at his side and took the lead in setting their direction. "Really?" he asked. "About what?"

"Everything," Jimmy said. "You don't know what it's like. It's a big mess. My grandma died, and Dave and Jacob left, and I keep getting in trouble, and . . . I didn't know it would be like this."

"Be like *what?* What're you talking about?"

"You know," Jimmy said, "being a Christian."

"I could've told you that was a dumb idea," Tony said.

"I don't know if it's a mistake. I mean . . ." Jimmy faltered. "Oh, I don't know what I mean."

"You're saying it's not all it's cracked up to be, right?"

Jimmy thought about it for a moment, then said, "Right."

"So why don't you give it up?" Tony asked. "You joined the club, and now you wanna unjoin it. It's not against the law."

"I know, but—"

"Looks to me like it's nothing but trouble. You never punched me in the nose before," Tony said with a laugh.

Jimmy smiled and answered, "Huh uh. And . . . you know, I'm . . . you know."

"Forget about it."

Jimmy looked at Tony and couldn't imagine why he thought he could give him up as a friend. "Tony, I—" He stopped himself when he noticed where they had walked to: the gazebo.

"What're we doing here?" Jimmy asked.

"Just walking," Tony said. "So, what're you going to do? Are you gonna keep doing this Sunday school stuff, or are you gonna get things back to the way they used to be?"

"I don't know, Tony," Jimmy said.

"I think you have to make up your mind. A lot of the kids at school are talking about you. They think you're weird. Some of the guys are saying you're a tattletale."

"Huh?"

"I don't believe it, but they're saying you told what happened with the firecrackers. Did you tell anybody?"

"No!" Jimmy said, then remembered he had confessed everything to Dave and Jacob and then his parents. "Oh . . ."

"You *did*, didn't you?"

"Only Dave—and then my parents," Jimmy said.

"You got us in trouble," Tony said, his voice stiffening.

"How? We've been gone! My dad didn't say anything to anybody."

Tony poked Jimmy in the chest with his finger. "Yeah," he accused, "but it turns out your friend Dave played racquetball with one of the guys from my dad's office, and he told him all about the firecrackers. My dad found out, and he was furious. So we all got in trouble—and there'll be more trouble later."

Out of the corner of his eye, Jimmy saw Gary walk around from behind the gazebo. Then Tim came around the other side. Cory stepped out from behind a tree and headed toward them. Jimmy didn't know for certain what they planned to do, but he figured it wouldn't be very nice.

"Look, Jimmy," Tony said, "as long as you wanna keep playing the religious nut and getting us in trouble, we don't wanna be your friends anymore. Okay?"

At that moment, Jimmy knew that if he promised Tony and the guys that he would quit being a Christian, they might leave him alone. Maybe they could be friends again and do things the way they did before. At that moment, it was possible. At that moment, it was a serious consideration. But at that moment, Jimmy couldn't make such a promise and decided on another course of action. . . .

Run!

He pushed Tony and took off as fast as he could. He made it as far as the path into the woods before one of the kids tackled him. Then they were all on him with wild, flying fists that didn't hit hard but connected with enough places on his face and body to hurt. Jimmy swung back just as wildly, but it didn't help.

Someone slugged him in the stomach. It knocked the wind out of him. He gasped as the fists kept coming.

He barely heard the deep and powerful voice that commanded the kids to stop. The fists—and the boys connected to them—withdrew, scattered, and ran off in several directions through the woods.

Strong hands lifted Jimmy to a sitting position. "Take it easy, Jimmy. Breathe slowly. Slowly."

Jimmy tried to take in some air. A handkerchief was pressed against his nose and lip. "You're bleeding a little. Can you stand up?" the deep voice asked.

"I think so," Jimmy croaked.

"Good. My shop is right over here. Come on."

Jimmy looked up into the face of his rescuer. It was John Avery Whittaker.

CHAPTER TWENTY

Sunday Evening

J ohn Avery Whittaker—or Whit, as a lot of people called him—owned a soda shop and discovery emporium on the edge of McAlister Park. He called it Whit's End. It was a popular gathering place for kids and adults, with room after room of exhibits, interactive displays, a library, and a theater. Whit was dedicated to anything that would help bring the Bible to life for kids. Jimmy went there on occasion with his parents. He didn't go more often because Tony didn't like it.

"I don't open on Sundays," Whit explained as he unlocked the front door. "But we should get some ice on that nose of yours."

He led Jimmy past the soda counter, into the kitchen, and over to a chair next to a small table. He disappeared into a walk-in freezer and returned a few seconds later with a clump of ice. He methodically broke it up with an ice pick, wrapped it in a cloth, and gently placed it so that it covered the side of Jimmy's nose and upper lip.

"Ow!" Jimmy said. His nose and lip throbbed.

"Just tilt your head back and hold it there while I call your parents," Whit said. "What's your number?"

Jimmy told him. Whit went to the phone and had a brief conversation with George. He hung up, then turned back to Jimmy. "Your dad's on his way," he said. He grabbed a chair and pulled it up close. "Do you want to tell me what that was all about? I assume you weren't being robbed."

"No," Jimmy replied. "Do I have to say who did it?"

"Not if you don't want to," Whit said.

Jimmy thought for a moment, then said, "I don't know where to start."

"Why did they beat you up?"

"Because I became a Christian."

Whit cocked an eyebrow quizzically. "I heard about that. But I didn't think kids got beat up for it around Odyssey."

"They do." Jimmy sighed. "Mr. Whittaker, I became a Christian, and it's ruined everything. I'm driving my family crazy, I lost my best friend, my grandmother died, and Dave and Jacob left."

Whit nodded slowly as if he understood completely. "I knew about Dave and Jacob. But I didn't know you were so close to them."

"Dave was the one who talked me into becoming a Christian, and Jacob helped me this week," Jimmy explained, then sighed again. "It's all gone wrong."

"So being a Christian isn't what you thought it would be?" Whit asked, echoing the question Jimmy was asked earlier.

"I guess not. I thought things would get better, and they didn't."

Whit took the ice pack, adjusted it a little, and put it back against Jimmy's face. "How did you think things would get better?"

"I thought that Jesus was going to change me—take everything, make it better, then give it back nice and new."

"I see," Whit said thoughtfully. "And you thought it would happen right away."

Jimmy shrugged. "Maybe not right away. Dave kept saying I had to be patient. But I didn't think everything would go wrong while I was being patient."

"So why don't you give it up?"

Surprised, Jimmy looked at Whit. It was the last thing he thought Whit would ask.

Whit chuckled and said, "Well, why don't you?"

"Because . . ." Jimmy began, but he didn't know how to go further. Finally he blurted, "Because I *can't.*"

"Why not?"

"Because my mom and dad would be upset," Jimmy stammered.

"I thought they were upset with you already. What's the difference?"

"It's a different *kind* of upset," Jimmy explained. "*That's* the difference. See, now they're upset because I keep making dumb mistakes. Before they were upset because I kept doing things to get in trouble."

Whit's eyes lit up with laughter. His white moustache spread across his round face. "That's wonderful!" he said. "I've never heard it explained so well. So you're telling me you became a Christian to please your parents?"

"No . . ."

"Then what were you thinking when you did it? I mean, I'm sorry you had a bad week. And I'm *deeply* sorry you lost your grandmother. Because of her poor health, though, I think you would've lost her whether you became a Christian or not. So I don't understand why you think it all connects to your becoming a believer."

Jimmy thought about it for a moment. "It connects because it happened after I said yes to Jesus."

"Because you thought He'd make everything all right when you said yes. Is that it?"

Jimmy nodded. That was it in a nutshell. He thought Jesus would make everything all right, and instead everything went wrong.

"Do you know what I think?" Whit asked. "I think everything *is* connected. It makes perfect sense—*if* you think about how God works sometimes."

"What do you mean?"

"Jimmy, God loves you more than anyone in this world ever could. He loves you so much that He sent Jesus to die for you. But Jesus didn't die so you could walk around with a smile on your face or so you'd never have a problem. The fact is, He died so you could be friends with God; so you could learn to love God the best you can; so you could be *changed* into the person He wants you to be. Do you understand that much?"

Jimmy said he did. It was another way of saying what Dave had said the night Jimmy became a Christian.

"Here's the next part," Whit continued. "Jesus' death didn't come easily, and neither does our change. It's a struggle, a battle, against all the things inside us that want everything to stay the way it was. That's why we make a lot of mistakes. We do things we know better than to do. Our family might get annoyed at us. And I'm not surprised that your friends have turned against you, though I'm a little surprised they went as far as knocking you around. They want to keep you the way you were. But Jesus is inside you now and wants you to fight to be more and more like Him. Are you still with me?"

Jimmy nodded again.

Whit went on, choosing his words carefully. "Sometimes . . . God strips away the things in our lives that keep us from relying on Him."

A light went on in Jimmy's head, and he sat up straight.

Whit noticed Jimmy's change in expression but slowly went on. "Sometimes God strips away the things we think are important to make room for us to see Him more clearly. Only then can He make the changes He needs to make. That's what growth is all about. And, yes, sometimes it hurts as we lose friends or suffer the loss of those we love. Sometimes we feel completely alone and figure that no one else in the whole wide world knows how we feel.

"But that's wrong. God knows. And that's why you're never alone. God is there, first and foremost. Then there's your family—who love you even when you get on their nerves. And then there are friends you have who are Christians—or the friends you haven't made yet. Like me, Jimmy. I'm always here if you need to talk."

"Thanks," Jimmy said softly and hung his head.

"Oh, now, Jimmy," Whit said with a smile. "Don't be too hard on yourself. You're only at the *start* of this new adventure. It's bound to be overwhelming for you."

"You never met my grandmother, did you?" Jimmy asked.

"I don't think so. Why?"

"Because she said the same things you just said," Jimmy answered.

"She must've been a very wise woman," Whit said, chuckling.

"Yeah," Jimmy said. "I'm going to miss her a lot."

Whit took the ice pack from Jimmy and looked closely at his wounds. "Just remember, Jimmy," he said, "that God never takes anything out of our lives unless He's going to replace it with something else—something that will help us the same way or more. You just have to keep your eyes open for it."

Whit pressed the ice pack against Jimmy's face again. Jimmy looked into his eyes and saw heartfelt kindness looking back. *I need to hang around Whit's End a lot more*, he decided.

CHAPTER TWENTY-ONE

Monday

Jimmy sat down at a lunch table with his tray of food. At another table across the room, he saw Tony and his old friends laughing at a joke Jimmy would never be a part of again. He wished he could be friends with them. But at this point in his life, he didn't know how. He closed his eyes, said a quick prayer of thanks for the food, and hoped no one saw him.

He opened his mouth to take the first bite of his pot roast, and his lip stung. It was a cruel reminder of the day before. There wasn't a lot of swelling on his face, but it still hurt a little. "Okay, God," he prayed, "it's just me alone at this table with a face that hurts. But it'll be all right if You'll help me." He sighed. It had been another bad day so far.

Jack Davis came up to Jimmy's table with a brown lunch bag in hand. "Hi, Jimmy," he said. "Okay if I sit down?"

Jimmy shrugged. He was afraid Jack had come over to tease him.

"What happened to your face?" Jack asked.

Jimmy self-consciously glanced over at Tony.

Jack must have noticed, because he said, "Never mind. You don't have to tell me." He shook his head and continued, "Boy, you've really been through it."

"What do you mean?" Jimmy asked.

"I dunno. It seems like a lot's happened to you lately. I've never seen a kid go through the wringer like that." Jack bit into his sandwich. He kept talking, even with a mouth full of food. "I guess you and Tony are on the outs, huh?"

"Yeah," Jimmy said, wondering what Jack might be up to.

Jack silently chewed his food, swallowed, then said softly, "That happened to me—y'know, being friends one minute, then not being friends the next. You remember Colin."

Jimmy did. He was a kid Jack had befriended who turned out to be an uncontrollable liar.

"Anyway, I was thinking that I know how you feel," Jack said. Then he stayed silent for a while.

Jimmy gazed at Jack while Jack looked down at his potato chips. Could they be friends? Jimmy wondered. Did God send him over to be a replacement for Tony, as Whit said? But there was no way to replace Tony or the years they had as friends, any more than his grandmother could be replaced.

That didn't mean, however, that God couldn't bring someone *new* into his life.

"Jimmy," Jack said, and Jimmy was suddenly embarrassed for staring at him.

"Yeah?"

"I saw you at the club meeting that night, and then I heard a rumor that you became a Christian."

"So?"

Jack scrunched his face up as if he didn't know how to ask what he wanted to ask. "Well, I was wondering . . . I mean, what's going on? I think about Jesus sometimes because, you know, my parents are Christians, but . . . I can't make up my mind about what it means."

Jimmy looked at Jack intently. "You want to know Jesus? I can tell you how to get to know Him. But it isn't easy, and it isn't always fun. In fact, right now it hurts more than anything I've ever done in my life. But you know what? It's all there is . . . and I wouldn't trade it for anything. Jesus'll get me through this. I don't know how, but He will."

"I figured you'd say something like that." Jack smiled and paused. "Y'know, me and Oscar and Lucy are going to Whit's End after school today. You wanna come with us?"

"I'll ask my parents," Jimmy said.

The day didn't seem so bad after that.

Don't Miss a Single "Adventures in Odyssey" Novel!

Strange Journey Back
Mark Prescott hates being a newcomer in the small town of Odyssey. And he's not too thrilled about his only new friend being a girl. That is, until Patti tells him about a time machine called The Imagination Station at Whit's End. With hopes of using the machine to bring his separated parents together again, Mark learns a valuable lesson about friendship and responsibility.

High Flyer with a Flat Tire
Joe Devlin is accusing Mark of slashing the tire on his new bike. Mark didn't do it, but how can he prove his innocence? Only by finding the real culprit! With the help of his wise friend, Whit, Mark untangles the mystery and learns new lessons about friendship and family ties.

The Secret Cave of Robinwood
Mark promises his friend Patti he will never reveal the secret of her hidden cave. But when a gang Mark wants to join is looking for a new clubhouse, Mark thinks of the cave. Will he risk his friendship with Patti? Through the adventure, Mark learns about the need to belong and the gift of forgiveness.

Behind the Locked Door
Why does Mark's friend Whit keep his attic door locked? What's hidden up there? While staying with Whit, Mark grows curious when he's forbidden to go behind the locked door. It's a hard-learned lesson about trust and honesty.

Lights Out at Camp What-a-Nut
At camp, Mark finds out he's in the same cabin with Joe Devlin, Odyssey's biggest bully. And when Mark and Joe are paired in a treasure hunt, they plunge into unexpected danger and discover how God uses one person to help another.

The King's Quest
Mark is surprised and upset to find he must move back to Washington, D.C. He feels like running away. With Whit's help, he uses The Imagination Station to go on a quest for a king to retrieve a precious ring. Through the journey, Mark faces his fears and learns the importance of obeying authority and striving for eternal things.

Danger Lies Ahead
Things in Odyssey have been a little strange lately—especially with rumors of an escaped convict heading for town! Jack makes a new friend, but something suspicious is going on. In wondering whom to trust, he learns to be careful when choosing friends.

About the Author

Paul McCusker is producer, writer, and director for the Adventures in Odyssey audio series. He is also the author of a variety of popular plays including *The First Church of Pete's Garage*, *Pap's Place*, and co-author of *Sixty-Second Skits* (with Chuck Bolte).

Other Works by the Author

NOVELS:
> *Strange Journey Back* (Focus on the Family)
> *High Flyer with a Flat Tire* (Focus on the Family)
> *The Secret Cave of Robinwood* (Focus on the Family)
> *Behind the Locked Door* (Focus on the Family)
> *Lights Out at Camp What-a-Nut* (Focus on the Family)
> *The King's Quest* (Focus on the Family)
> *Danger Lies Ahead* (Focus on the Family)

INSTRUCTIONAL:
> Youth Ministry Comedy & Drama:
>> *Better Than Bathrobes But Not Quite Broadway*
>> (with Chuck Bolte; Group Books)

PLAYS:
> *Pap's Place* (Lillenas)
> *A Work in Progress* (Lillenas)
> *Snapshots & Portraits* (Lillenas)
> *Camp W* (Contemporary Drama Services)
> *Family Outings* (Lillenas)
> *The Revised Standard Version of Jack Hill* (Baker's Plays)
> *Catacombs* (Lillenas)
> *The Case of the Frozen Saints* (Baker's Plays)
> *The First Church of Pete's Garage* (Baker's Plays)

SKETCH COLLECTIONS:
> *Short Skits for Youth Ministry* (with Chuck Bolte; Group Books)
> *Sixty-Second Skits* (with Chuck Bolte; Group Books)
> *Void Where Prohibited* (Baker's Plays)
> *Fast Food* (Monavah Books)
> *Quick Skits & Discussion Starters* (with Chuck Bolte; Group Books)
> *Vantage Points* (Lillenas)
> *Batteries Not Included* (Baker's Plays)
> *Souvenirs* (Baker's Plays)
> *Sketches of Harvest* (Baker's Plays)

MUSICALS:
> *A Time for Christmas* (Word)
> *Shine the Light of Christmas* (Word)

Breakaway
With colorful graphics, hot topics, and humor, this magazine for teen guys helps them keep their faith on course and gives the latest info on sports, music, celebrities . . . even girls. Best of all, this publication shows teens how they can put their Christian faith into practice and resist peer pressure.

Clubhouse
Here's a fun way to instill Christian principles in your children! With puzzles, easy-to-read stories, and exciting activities, *Clubhouse* provides hours of character-building enjoyment for kids ages 8 to12.

All magazines are published monthly except where otherwise noted. For more information regarding these and other resources, please call Focus on the Family at (719) 531-5181, or write to us at Focus on the Family, Colorado Springs, CO 80995.